Night Walkers

Brionna Paige McClendon

When you are given the choice of eternal life, would you accept?

The Beginning
Chapter One

The thick, warm liquid cascaded down my throat like a bloody waterfall. The taste of it was like the sweetest of nectars. My mind soared with bliss, my body thrummed in ecstasy. The blood dripped from the corners of my lips, my tongue slipped from my mouth and licked at the escaped liquid. It burned my tongue with its too sweet flavor. I craved more, so much more. My thirst could never be satisfied, no matter how many victims fell at my feet, still more I craved. My hunger was yet to be filled. My fangs sunk deeper into my victim's neck causing more blood to pour into my mouth. Down it fell in my throat, burning on its way down into my stomach. The beast inside me was awakening, I could feel it as it clawed at my damned soul. The victim in my grasp was slipping away from this life, their soul would carry on to the next. A moan escaped them, but it was not a moan of pain. No. It was a moan of pleasure. This was like a high for them, the effect of a vampire's bite. Some called it Vampire's Kiss, naming it like it was some sort of drug created by the human race. Fools. Many of them didn't live long enough to tell the tale of the *"Vampire's Kiss"*.

As of now, the one who could speak of the tale is slowly slipping away. The life disappearing from their eyes but they weren't aware of what was happening. They were soaring to new heights, floating across lands, swimming in vast oceans. Their mind playing harsh tricks on them, making them believe they would live to see the new dawn. But, sadly they would not. I felt remorse for some of my victims. But not all, many deserved to die. Rapists, child molesters, murderers. I chuckled at the last one, for I was a murderer myself. I relished in the pain I afflicted upon those horrible people. Sucking the life from their veins. I made sure they knew they were dying, slowly. But the man I held in my arms now, I did not want him to be aware that his life was leaving him. I had convinced him he was safe from harm, lured him here into my arms. The power of a vampire's voice could be *very* convincing but our ageless beauty also was a factor at play.

Feeding time was coming to an end as the last drop of my victim's blood rolled across my tongue and fell down my throat, burning on its way down into my stomach. The man's hazel eyes glazed over as his soul slipped away from his body. I could have saved him, stopped my feeding, turned him into a monster like me. But I did not wish to bring upon him an eternity of never ending life. An endless cycle of unfulfilled life, an undead immortal walking amongst the living. He would be forced to watch as his loved ones grew old and withered away. Many humans declined the gift of immortal life, I would not call it a gift more of a curse.

Staring into the dead man's eyes, I noted the flecks of gold that scattered throughout his irises. The brown rings on the outer portion of his eyes and the green that circled around his pupils. In a past life, my eyes were the same as his but now they were blue. A blue that was ghostly and caused humans to question what I was. The blue was too odd. Human eyes were never this shade of blue. Many thought of my eyes as things of beauty and wonder. However, during feeding time, when my fangs revealed themselves, the color of my eyes would shift to a deep and dark crimson. Much like the color of blood. This held true for every vampire.

"Princess Nehemiah. Is your feeding time finished?" A servant entered into the feeding room. She approached me with her hands held behind her back. She was still new, a fledgling vampire. That being why her eyes were as red as the blood moon, a few more days and they would turn blue. Nervousness spilled from her being, I could understand her nerves. Being in the presence of a royal and an old vampire could stir the nerves of any immortal. Any that had fear to feel that is.

A sigh escaped my messy blood coated lips as I peered at the man by my feet. "Yes, I am finished."

Hurrying over to the body, she hefted it over her shoulder and disappeared behind a door. That door led into the room where we deposited the bodies of the dead humans. Held within that room were vampires who committed crimes against our kind, their meals were the bloodless bodies. Nothing but bones would be left of the victims. It was just enough to keep them breathing, barely. For their crimes this was the fate they deserved, imprisoned for the rest of their long, long lives. As the door opened I could hear their snarls of hunger and anger. The servant girl returned, seeming disturbed having to witness the criminals of our kind. I could only imagine how they appeared now, scrawny and boney things. Their beauty stolen away from them. I had hoped that having to look upon them, it would keep her inline and abide by our laws. Seeing a pretty thing like her turn to nothing but skin and bones would be such a waste of beauty.

Her face was round with youngness. She was sixteen when she died and came back as a fledgling. She was only five-foot-three in height. Her golden hair fell to her shoulders in bouncy ringlets, much like a southern belle. Those crimson eyes of hers were off putting to her innocent looks and nature. To many she would appear helpless, defenseless but that was far from it. Vampires were stronger than any human. We could leap buildings in one bound. Soar high into the skies. Control the weak minds of humans. Our senses were that of a predatory bird, our eyes and ears sharp and attuned to everything around us. We were the superior race compared to the frailness of the humans.

"Queen Persephone, wishes to speak with you." Her voice was shaken.

The queen was called by many names; Queen of the Dead, Queen of Vampires, Ruler of the Under World, Harbinger of Souls. But those few of us who were born from her bite, called her mother. The one who brought us into this new life. I was the first child she ever turned, eight hundred years ago I started anew.

It was nightfall, the sun sunk below the horizon many hours before allowing the moon time to shine with its greatness. Mother warned me to stay inside at night but of course I never listened to my mother's paranoia. The life of night called to me every sunset of everyday. I enjoyed the sounds and calmness the evening brought with it. The sounds of the insects around me singing their songs, the coolness of the air caressing my skin gently. Seating myself upon the log I sat on every evening, I tilted my head back and admired the sky above me. Thousands and thousands of stars sprinkled across the blackness of the sky. The moon being their ruler, it was the ruler of the night. Claiming it for its own. The river before me rushed along, making sounds of splashing as it cascaded across the rocks of the bank. My mind and soul were at peace, fulfilled with happiness. A smile crossed my lips. And suddenly, the sound of a song swept past my ears. A woman's singing voice filled the quiet night with beauty. I was hypnotized by her harmony of the notes she sang. But, I could not understand the words that sung from her lips. A language I had not learned or heard before. Still, her voice was hauntingly beautiful. It sent chills along my spine causing my body to shudder. Then the singing woman came into sight. She stood on the other side of the river. Her body nude, completely exposed. I couldn't help but stare at her beauty, not only was her body worth admiration so was her face. It was slim with high cheeks bones that could cut through one's self confidence. Her brows were dark and thin. Her lips plump and a silky pink. Those midnight locks of hers cascaded down her back in waves and stopped at her ankles. Her dark hair contrasted well with the lightness of her skin, so pale it was. But her eyes were what truly drew me into her. They were blue but a very clear and haunting hue of it. Clearer than a cloudless sky. Something about her wasn't entirely human. She was too perfect for words. My mind could not comprehend what this woman was or could be. As she sang she stepped out onto the water of the river, walking across the surface of it. I wanted to fear this woman, no human could do such a thing, but something inside of me told me I was safe. A cool calmness washed over my being.

    Soon, the woman stood before me. Her eyes took me in. Seeming like she was considering something the way her brows creased with curiosity. She knelt before where I sat on the log, her hands taking mine. Her touch was cold and lifeless. Goosebumps arose on my arms. I found it hard to speak, to form words, like a spell had been casted on me. Then her lips moved as she spoke delicately, "What is your name, child?" Her voice was like music to my ears.

    "Alexandria." The word formed on my lips.

    "Alexandria, a fitting name for a human." Her ghostly eyes locked themselves with mine. "If I could offer you eternal life, would you accept?"

    My mind tried to grasp the words she spoke. I found it hard to comprehend. Eternal life? Could this be true? But as I looked into her eyes, I knew the words she spoke were no lie. Something about this woman was no longer human. "I would." Those words whispered from my lips.

    "Even if it meant leaving behind the life you know?"

I had not much of a life, a simple farm girl who lived with her deranged mother. That was the life I had and the life I had to look forward too. I had decided. "Yes."

"There shall be no going back, no returning to this life. I ask one last time, do you accept?" *Her eyes were wise, knowing. She knew what my answer was to be but she wanted me to voice it.*

"I accept."

She exhaled a breath and stood before me. Leaning her head back in the moon's light she opened her mouth revealing a row of pearly white, straight teeth. Then, two long sharpened teeth grew from either side of her two front teeth. Matching her gaze with mine once more, I found that her eyes were no longer blue but a deep red. Still, I should have felt fear but I did not fear this woman. Why? I do not know. She knelt down to me, brushed my short black hair away from my neck, and placed her moist lips to my skin. Her sharpened teeth brushed my skin and suddenly a pinch of pain took over me. Deeper those teeth of hers sank into my neck, I could feel a thick warm liquid dripping from the wound she created. The pain I felt was replaced with a warm feeling that spread like a fire throughout my veins. My mind was surrounded in a fog of blissfulness. Closing my eyes, a light moan escaped me. Was this what sex felt like? A flame burned inside of me. I felt like I was soaring in the clouds. My body thrummed with pleasure. Then, the woman removed her teeth from my neck. I fell into her arms and she lowered me to the ground in her lap. Staring into those eyes of hers they transformed color once again, I found myself looking into ghostly blue eyes. Then, she began to sing again. Luring me to sleep. And sleep I did.

My eyes closed and when I had wakened, I was new. Transformed. My body pulsated with strength. My ears were aware of all the sounds around me, even miles away. My eyes took in the new world around me. Seeing things that no human eye could see. The woman helped me to stand but I did not need the help. My scalp tingled with a strange sensation and then I noticed that my short hair began to grow. It grew and grew and stopped at my waist. Glancing down at my arms I saw the scars that I had accumulated from working on the farm, slowly began to fade away and nothing remained of them.

The woman stood before me with a smile on her perfect lips. "What are you?" I whispered into the night.

"Humans call me many things; witch, demon, dead woman of the living." She giggled. "But what my species is called is, Vampire."

Tales of creatures were spoken of in my small village. Creatures of the night, my people had given them the name of, Night Walkers. People who only came out at night, never did you see them during the day. "And now I am a vampire?" A stupid question for me to ask at the time. The answer was obvious.

"Yes, my child. You have been reborn, given a new life. You can choose a new name for yourself if you like."

I was given the name of my mother at birth. "Nehemiah. That is my new name."

A smile spread across her lips. "I knew you would choose that name. It's a very suiting name for you, my daughter." I blinked at her in surprise when she called me daughter. She laughed at this. "You are the first of my bloodline now. First of my name. Blood of my blood. I am the queen of vampires and now you, Nehemiah, are the princess of vampires."

From simple farm girl to princess of vampires. Everything was changing so fast. "What is your name?" I asked.

The woman held one of my hands, "Persephone. But you may call me mother." With that, she led me through the night. Led me away from the life I once knew. And led me to a new life. My new beginning.

Back then I did not realize that she had been tricking my human mind. Using my dislike for my mother and unsatisfying life to her advantage. She saw something in me that night when we first met one another. Did she change me into this creature for her own personal use?

Or for my own good? I still had yet to figure out which one rang true. Eight hundred years have passed since that fateful night and I have never left her side.

    My mind wondered with thoughts of the past as I traveled down the castle hallways. Paintings that were rich in detail hung from the stone walls. Paintings depicting the queen in all her glory. Others depicted gruesome battles between the vampires and humans, back in the olden days when they were made aware of our presence on this earth. All because of one foolish man of our kind, he is still chained up till this day behind the door in the feeding room. Because of him we were almost put to extinction. The man should have been chained up and made to wait till sunrise and burn in its light. But the queen thought it more fitting to have him locked away for all eternity. She told me I was too quick to sentence one to death but death he deserved.

    Soon I found myself entering into the queen's personal chambers. My hand pushed open the thick wooden door to reveal the queen standing before her floor length mirror, naked. Shutting the door behind me I approached the woman. Her ghostly eyes stared upon her own reflection. Her midnight hair swept across the floor. A warm smile tugged at her lips when I appeared in the reflection behind her.

    "Greetings, my child."

    "The servant girl, Selene, said you wished to see me."

    Walking over to her bed she grabbed a robe that was resting upon it. Slipping the velvet red robe on she said, "Ah, yes. We have trouble with the hunters again. A small group was spotted in the forest on the west side of the castle."

    "Would you like for me to arrange a small group and send them after the hunters?"

    She peered over her shoulder at me with a mischievous smile on her lips. "No. I would like for you to take care of them for me, my daughter."

    The queen knew I was more than capable of taking on a group of vampire hunters, a group of ten I could take down easily in a span of a few minutes. Being the first of her blood, I was the strongest of her children. Nodding my head to her I said, "Consider it done."

As I approached the door she called out to me, "Oh and Nehemiah my child, bring their bodies to the feeding room. Tonight we feast."

Making my way down the hallway and down the staircase that led into the entry room of the castle I approached the two massive doors. Two vampire men stood beside the door on guard. They were both very handsome, but so was every other vampire man to walk this earth. Both of them turned their attention to me and nodded their heads. Pushing open the doors I walked out into the cold winter's night. The freezing weather did not bother me, I could spend the night out here nude and live. Snow crunched under my feet as I walked across the snow covered bridge. Approaching the west side of the forest I stood in silence, listening to the sounds the night brought. I listened for the sound of hunters. My body was growing anxious waiting for the thrill of the hunt. Suddenly, I was thirsty for blood again. My throat burned for it. Soon the craving would be satisfied. My ears rang with the sound of hurried footsteps plowing through the deep snow. They were coming, for me. A wicked smile formed on my lips as I waited for the hunters to make an appearance. From the sound of the footsteps I knew there were five in this group. A laugh escaped me, child's play these hunters would prove to be.

The sound of an arrow whizzed through the air, my hand reached up in time to grab it just inches from my nose. A chuckle escaped me as I snapped the wooden arrow in my grasp. They had no idea who they were dealing with. The sound of steel slicing through air rang in my ears, dodging to the left I watched as a dagger flew past my face. Then another came flying at me from the darkness of the forest. Catching the blade between my fingers, I aimed it back into the forest after I listened close enough to pin point the thrower's position. The blade flew through the air in a blur and soon the sound of a heavy body hitting the ground sounded in my ears. One down, four to go. My body thrummed with excitement. Opening my mouth, I revealed my fangs. I felt them growing longer and stopping at sharp points. My tongue ran across them. The craving for blood intensified, burning like a blazing fire inside my throat. Then, four shadowy fingers stepped forth from behind the trees. In my ears rang the sound of each of their heartbeats, I could hear the blood roaring through their veins. Each heart had its own unique beat and pulse to it. It only urged my craving. My eyes could see that one of them was mourning the death of their fallen comrade. I could see the bloodshot veins in the whites of her eyes. The dried tear stains on her rosy cheeks. Hatred burned in those dark eyes of hers. Within her hands she held a bow and arrow, she was the shooter. I felt regret for killing the girl's comrade but that was quickly wiped away when I thought of how many vampires these people have killed.

 A girl stepped toward me with a sword in hand. Her brunet hair was pulled back into a high ponytail. Her face was hard with hate and murder. She would strike rashly without thought, that would prove fatal for her. Ending a life that was young with life to look forward too, saddened me. My life was ended young but I was born again into a killing beast. The girl rushed at me shouting out with anger, a battle cry. Her sword slashed through the empty air where I once stood. I found myself standing behind the young girl, fear perspired off of her body. It reeked foully in my nostrils. I hated the smell of fear. She wondered where I was, her training did not prepare her for me. I was not like the others. My hands gripped either side of her head and with a sharp crack, her neck was broken. Her body fell to the ground with a soft *thud*. Her heart ceased its beating.

 Three.

 Turning around I faced the other hunters. The girl holding a bow cried out as she watched her other comrade die by my hands. By now she writhed with hatred, it spilled out from her being and across the land. She would be the last to die, I decided. Next was a tall, muscular man. Mid-thirties, I guessed him at. His face was rugged, much like a mountain man. Spending his days chopping down trees. Which explained his well-toned arms and legs. His hair was chopped off revealing a cleanly shaven head. His eyes were determined. For that, I admired him. Fear was not what he felt. To him, I was just another vampire set to die at his hands. I would entertain this man. It would prove to be fun. His first attack was throwing a fist toward my face. Easily, I caught his fist in my hand. Locking my eyes with his I still saw no fear in his face. His training prepared him for death. Slowly I turned his wrist till it broke, the man's face contorted in pain. Reaching behind him he withdrew a wooden stake from his belt that was equipped with many weapons. He was a fool to think he would be quick enough to drive that through my heart. With a blur my hand stole the stake from his grasp and drove it deep into his chest. The man fell to his knees staring me deep in the eyes. "Damn you to hell." He spat.

Leaning down I whispered in a loving voice into his ear, "My soul is already damned."

He coughed up blood and fell down, landing on his side. The stake I had driven through his chest found its way through his back. The sharpened point had stabbed its way through his spine. Dark liquid wept from his wound and painted the snowy ground in crimson. I fought back my urge to feed, now was not the time. His eyes glossed over. I had hoped his soul would be damned just like mine. He killed many of my kind, for that he deserved to be condemned to the underworld.

Two.

Next, was another man. A man much younger than the one before, early twenties. This one was not as muscular as the last, he was rather scrawny. A twig of a thing. I could easily snap his body in half. A smile tugged at my lips picturing it in my mind. Envisioning the sounds of his bones cracking. My hunger was burning. I needed to satisfy this craving soon and I would. Just two hunters remained. Striding up to the young man, I had a devious plan in mind. Young men loved beautiful women. They were easy to manipulate. Holding my chin high I walked with seduction pouring from my body. Swinging my hips just right. Teasing my prey sent a rush of thrill through my body. I could almost taste the ecstasy. Locking my eyes with his I put the young man in a trance. Now, he was mine. This trick I had learned from the queen. "What is your name, boy?"

"Martin." His voice was monotone, his eyes wide.

"Martin, do you think I'm beautiful?" I waltzed around him, trailing my fingertips across his shoulders and back.

"Yes."

A chuckle escaped me. My fingers gripped his chin forcing him to look down at me, down into my eyes. I watched him as he fell deeper into my hypnotizing gaze. "Martin, kiss me. I know you want too." My voice dripped with innocence.

Lowering his head, his lips met with mine. The kiss was wet and sloppy but that wouldn't bother me for much longer. I deepened the kiss, sealing my lips around his. Slowly, I began to suck the life away from the man. Vampires could kiss a mortal without killing them but that took years of training, we were far too strong. I could control it but tonight, I would not. As I sucked the life from his lungs his body began to fight me but not for long. Soon he fell to the ground with that hypnotized look still fresh in his eyes. Stepping over the corpse I faced the young girl before me. She had stood and watched as I killed her friends off one by one. Tears brimmed in her dark brown eyes. They reminded me of chocolate. Her pretty face was creased with grief and anger.

"One."

The young woman hunter raised her bow to me, fixing an arrow aimed at my chest. Did she not learn from her failed first attack? A chuckle escaped me as she let go of the arrow. I caught it in my grasp easily and tossed it down to the snowy ground. She reached back and drew forth another arrow from her quiver. This one would not learn, stubborn creature's humans were. There was only one hunter left they would have been more of a challenge if they had combined their strengths instead of attacking one by one. Fools. Had their training been for nothing? It seemed as though they were not prepared for me.

Maybe these people were a fresh batch of newbies sent out to test me.

"You will die by my hand you bitch from hell!" The woman finally spoke up.

"You are sadly mistaken, for you see, you will be the one to die." I strode up to the girl, bringing myself face to face with her. And as I stared into those eyes of hers, I was reminded of my mother. Even the woman's hair was the same fiery red that my mother's was. Leaning in closer to her I filled my nostrils with her scent, searching for a smell that I knew. And I found it. Taking a step back I looked at the woman, studied her. She was from my mother's bloodline. Though it has been eight hundred years I still remembered my mother's scent. My mother's blood coursed through this woman's veins, even though there might only be a small trace amount, I knew it was there. This hunter that stood before me was my family. It is true that I resented the woman whom gave birth to me but seeing this young woman before me now made it hard to kill her. It was as though she was the only small thing I had left of my mother. For a moment it seemed as though the old life I had flashed before my eyes. For some reason, I had missed that old farm and even my crazy mother. Instead of killing the woman I chose a fate for her that would go against who she was.

Forcefully I threw her against a tree. Her back slammed into it, knocking the breath from her lungs. Laying on the ground she struggled for air, gasping for it. Two of her ribs had been broken. She writhed in pain. Kneeling before the woman I brought her up into my lap, she was in too much pain to fight me. Humans were such fragile things, like glass. Pathetic really. Brushing her fiery hair away from her neck I sunk my fangs deep into her skin. The taste of blood poured into my mouth. But the taste of this blood sickened me. My mother's blood was in this woman's veins and I was drinking it. It felt wrong, so very wrong. Biting my tongue, I transferred my blood into her veins. I hurried with my bite and pulled away from the woman's bleeding neck. Soon, she would die and soon she would be reborn. The queen allowed each of her children to turn five people. The woman before me now would be my first, my child. First of my blood.

"W-What have you done to me?" Her hand reached up to her bleeding wound and her eyes gazed upon her crimson soaked fingers.

Leaning down I placed a kiss upon the woman's brow before whispering, "Now, you will become the creature you hate most on this earth." Standing and turning my back to her I said one last thing before leaving her there, "Welcome to your new life, *my daughter*."

Feeding Time
Chapter Two

Carrying the corpses of the four hunters on my shoulders I returned to the castle. The two men guarding the door offered to help me but I did not need help. I was stronger than the two men combined, that they knew. All they wanted was a night with me and they thought kindness was a way into my undead, frozen heart. I scoffed at the idea of laying with them. Yes, I have had my fair share of lovers but that has since come to an end. My earlier years were filled with blood and passion. Being a vampire stops you from having children and prevents you from contracting a disease. My young self-took advantage of that. At times I laid with more than one man at a time, even women. But those days are long since gone, locked away in my vault of memories.

Approaching the feeding room I dumped the bodies upon the dark marble flooring. Blood still poured from the man hunter, every vampire in this castle would go into a frenzy searching for the scent of human blood. Shutting the door behind me I ventured up to the queen's room. I knocked once before entering, I found her upon her bed making love to another woman, a servant girl. I was thankful that it was not Selene. She was still too young yet, too freshly born. It would seem wrong for the queen to lie with her. This would not be my first time walking in on the queen doing such things, other times I have found her with a man. Once in a great while she would lure human men into her chamber, sleep with them and suck the blood from their veins as they made love.

The queen noticed my presence and addressed me, "Is the task finished?"

"Yes, mother." I said with a sound of pride.

A smile formed on her too perfect lips. "I knew you would not disappoint me, you never do." Fixing her gaze upon the servant girl she said, "Go and inform everyone that the feast will begin shortly."

"Yes, my queen." The girl slipped her clothing on and left the chamber in a hurry.

"Nehemiah, tell me, how many hunters were there?"

"Four." I lied.

"Such a small group. Perhaps they were scouting the castle, trying to find a way inside." She did not dress herself, when we fed we were naked. "Now my dear, go and ready yourself for tonight's feeding."

It was time for the group feast. Waltzing down the staircase I took pride in my body. Each step I took down caused my breasts to bounce. Turning into a vampire had enlarged them quite a few sizes up from what they were when I was a human. A great many things changed about me, my looks were more fair. My hair longer and shinier. My breasts and butt larger. The men as well approached the feeding room naked, their packages exposed for the women to judge. I cannot say the same for the men's bodily changes, their genitals did not enlarge when they were transformed. It's sad, really.

Almost every vampire in the castle joined in on the group feeding, all except the servants. Together we gathered in a circle around the corpses. The smell of blood filled my nostrils causing my mouth to water. My body was ready for the feeding. Anticipation clawed at my being. Queen Persephone made her entrance, entering the center of the circle she approached the dead bodies of the hunters. A smile formed on her lips, a smile that thought of the hunters as foolish humans, a smile that was ready to feast. Wicked, it was. Soon those beautiful lips of hers would be coated in blood.

"My children, tonight we feast on the blood of our enemy. Tonight we fill our bodies with their life force. These humans were fools to think that they could bring death upon us," Her ghostly eyes peered into all of ours as she walked around the bodies speaking, "But death had plans for them tonight, and the reaper of souls has collected its toll." The queen's voice was beautiful and haunting.

It was tradition for the queen to take first blood. Leaning down to the bloody body of the male hunter she revealed her fangs and sunk them deep into the neck. It was oddly beautiful watching her feed. The queen was one of perfection, so perfect she was that her looks instantly put humans under her trance. Male and female alike found themselves hypnotized by her unearthly beauty. Blood dripped from the corners of her lips and running along her chin, staining her porcelain skin in crimson. Lifting her head up and tilting it back her tongue ran across her bloody lips, licking the mess away from her mouth. Those fangs of hers dripped with blood. Her crimson eyes landed upon me, her finger called me forth. It was my turn to feed, then the group would join us. Kneeling before the queen she offered me the body she had drank from. Revealing my fangs, I took a bite on the other side of the man's neck. The steamy, rich blood filled my mouth. I had waited to taste this man's blood since my nostrils first caught its scent. It took much willpower to resist the urge to feed then and there. Finally, I could drink my fill. My mind exploded with bliss, with the feeling of ecstasy. Blood was our drug. But it was also what kept us alive. It burned my tongue and throat as it made its way down into my stomach. It was so sweet, so savory. My body wanted more, so much more. I wanted to feed on the other bodies, take all the blood for myself. But I knew I could not. When it came to blood, every vampire was selfish about sharing their feed but the queen made sure we all had our fill. Removing my fangs from the skin, I tilted my head back and swallowed the mouthful of blood. Down it burned in my throat. My taste buds went wild once the blood swept across my tongue. The queen's face was right before my eyes, a flicker of pride flashed in her crimson eyes. But soon a frenzied look crossed her ageless face. It was group feeding time.

Calling out she said, "My people, it is feeding time!"

The vampires broke the circle formation and swarmed around us. Several vampires bit into one body at once, sucking away at the blood. Moans soon filled the feeding room as the vampires were becoming drunk on the savory liquid. Moving to another corpse I found myself sharing it with a handsome man. His crimson eyes locked themselves with mine as we fed on the blood. My body thrummed with pleasure. A moan escaped my blood coated lips. The vampire man took my face in his hands and forced a kiss upon me. I tasted the blood that filled his mouth and covered his soft lips. My mind exploded with excitement. My fingernails grew long and sharp and they sliced open the victim's body that lay before us. Dipping my fingers into the warm liquid I smeared it across the vampire's lips. His tongue licked at the substance. Forcing my lips against his once again my tongue made its way into his mouth, savoring the left over taste of blood. My mind was soaring away into the clouds, my soul drifting along the wind. The man broke the kiss and grabbed my blood soaked hand, his mouth formed around my bloody fingers sucking the thick liquid off of my skin. I felt as his tongue licked away at my fingers, his saliva washing away the blood.

Loud moans of pleasure rang out in the room. These were not moans of blood feeding, no. These were moans of lovemaking.

Glancing over to my right, I saw a female vampire making love with two other men. They were all soaked in blood. The men licked at the liquid that coated the woman's fair skin. She was drowning in ecstasy, in the savory taste of the blood. Her mind was absorbed in pleasure. During feedings, I did not participate in the lovemaking part. I no longer craved the intimacy of another. Often times after sex, I found myself feeling lost. A feeling of regret would wrap itself around my being. The void in my heart growing. Sure, it was fun at first but slowly it became tiresome. It had been nearly two hundred years since I last made love to another and I did not know when or if I ever would do such again. The male vampire that I had locked lips with knew that I did not do such at feedings, so he moved on to another who would. This did not hurt my feelings in the slightest, if I wanted to make love with him, I could. He joined with the two men and woman. A chuckle escaped me as I made my way over to another corpse. The corpse of the girl who's neck I had snapped as if it were a twig. Grabbing her arm, I sunk my fangs deep into her wrist. The blood was almost completely drained from the body. The last ounce of it trickled down my throat. Gazing around me I saw that each of the bodies were now drained of their blood. Feeding time has come to an end.

    After we piled the bodies on top of each other, we left the feeding room. The servants quickly filed in behind us ready to clean up the mess and dispose of the bodies. Feeding the corpses to the criminals. Selene was the last to enter, our gazes locked for a brief moment before she disappeared into the room. Returning to my own chamber, I decided to bathe. Blood was caked onto my skin, hardened. It was time to wash it off. When blood became stale it was no longer appetizing to vampires. We liked it fresh from the veins. My body sunk into the steaming water. The blood that encased my skin was washed away. My midnight hair fanned out across the water's surface around me. My body had its fill of blood, for now. I wouldn't hunger for it again for another few days after a feeding like that. Though vampires craved blood constantly we could go days and weeks without drinking even a drop of it. But if we went too long without feeding then it would prove fatal for us.

As I was stepping out of the bath a familiar scent wafted into my nostrils. I stood there, searching for the smell. Walking over to the balcony, I peered down over the metal railing. Far off into the distance I saw a woman with fiery hair standing between snow covered trees. A smirk crossed my lips as I leapt down from the balcony and landed on the heels of my feet in the snow. Approaching the woman, I sensed anger burning like a flame inside of her. Confusion also flickered off of her being. She was a fledgling vampire, an hour old. Her crimson eyes shone in the moon's light. And on her face I caught the sight of smeared blood on the corner of her mouth. She had already had her first feeding, but of what? Animal or human? Grasping her face in my hand I sniffed at the blood. Human. My eyebrow raised in question. There were no humans around here for miles. So where did she get her meal? Then, it clicked in my brain. Releasing my hold on her face a laugh escaped me.

"How ironic it is, the hunter becoming the monster they hunted. Tell me, why did you kill your own comrades?" She had killed them, once a fledgling vampire had a taste of blood there was no stopping them. They went into a frenzy until they had their fill.

Her face hardened. "When I returned to them they tried to kill me."

Once again I raised my eyebrow to her. "You were once a hunter. Wouldn't you wish to die since now you are the vampire that you feared?"

Her head shook. Her feelings were mixed. Confused. Part of her wished to die but the other part wished to live. The living part was winning. "I did not wish to die but I did not wish to be turned into a monster like you."

A scoff escaped me as I circled around the woman. "You are living but you are also dead."

"What does that mean?"

Facing her again I said, "It means just the way it sounds. A dead thing breathing and walking amongst the living."

"Dead but also alive." Those words whispered quietly from her lips.

She was my responsibility now, my child. Blood of my blood. I did not know entirely the reason why I chose her. I should have killed her. Maybe my mother's bloodline played a role in my choosing. No, it was no maybe. That was the reason. This woman before me now was the only connection I had left of my crazed mother. She was family.

"Does the name Alexandria Hart, ring any bells to you?"

Her crimson eyes met with mine. She knew the name. But did she know of the woman? "I have heard of that name before. The hunters speak of her all the time."

My attention was fully on the woman, "Why?"

"She was the first of many vampire hunters. My bloodline stems from her, dating back generations."

For the first time, in a long time, I was lost for words. My mind was like a whirlwind as I tried to piece together my past life. Things began to make sense. The demons my mother spoke of were vampires. The reason she never wanted me out at night was to keep me safe. Her craziness was brought on by her job as a hunter. She was already mentally unstable after father left us alone when I was only four. Now, I understood my mother's actions. Regret clawed at me, sorrow, and grief. I felt stupid, I should have pieced the puzzle together sooner. The woman was a hunter from my mother's bloodline. Was I really so blind to the facts that were laid out before me? Eight hundred years later I finally figured out why mother acted the way she did.

"You look very much like her." The words escaped me as I stared upon the woman before me. It was like she was an exact reincarnation of my dead mother.

Her eyebrow raised in question. "How do you know what she looks like?"

A sigh escaped me, "Because, she was my mother. Eight hundred and eighteen years ago she gave birth to me." I did not count my human years as part of my age. When I died and was reborn, that was when my life truly started. Eight hundred years I have lived as a dead person walking amongst the living.

"A vampire hunter with a vampire child. Did she know you were turned?"

A sad chuckle left my lips, "She probably figured it out when I disappeared and never returned."

The sadness of reality hit me like a bullet. If my mother had found out what I was, she would have killed me. Being her daughter she would have been the one to put me down. No one else. I was her responsibility and also her failure. After so many centuries my feelings of sadness and grief were catching up to me. The woman that stood before me seemed surprised as she studied my face.

"I did not know a vampire could cry." Such a stupid statement. Of course we could cry. But we chose not to. The back of my hand wiped away the one single tear that escaped my eye. The first tear I had cried in nearly three hundred years.

"Did you not cry when you killed your comrades?" My voice was harsh.

"I wanted too but I could not find it in myself to cry at the time. I was too busy feeding on them as if they were nothing but chunks of meat." The woman stepped toward me, "Here is where our paths part. I will no longer speak with you or anyone else of our kind." Her crimson eyes were serious but she would come back, eventually. And I would be waiting.

As she turned her back to me and began to walk away I called out to her, "We will meet again. Whether it be ten years from now or a hundred. Our paths will cross once more."

Meeting Again
Chapter Three

One hundred and fifty-five years have passed since that night. The year was now twenty sixteen. The queen still resided in the same castle, as did the other vampires and I. Out of all the servants, Selene was still my favorite. Over the years we had become close friends. Selene was no longer a young fledgling, today was her one hundred and fifty fifth year living as a vampire. We did not celebrate birthdays unless it marked a thousand years of life. Forty-five more years and I would be celebrating my one thousandth year. As of now I was nine hundred and fifty-five.

Still, the queen had no clue of the first child I had created. I had not seen nor heard from her since that late winter's night. But this year, I had a strong feeling that our paths would cross once again. Fate, destiny, whatever you may call it, would draw us together. She was not dead, born of my blood line and trained as a hunter, she was a strong woman with the will to live. Anticipation ate away at my being throughout the day as I hid away in the castle from the sun's light.

    Though, I should have hated the woman, should have killed her. She was a hunter of my kind, my enemy. But I grew weak when I smelled my mother's blood in her veins. I had hoped my weakness would not come to make me regret the decision I had made. After piecing together my past life, all I could think about throughout the years was the fact that my mother was a vampire hunter. She had hidden away her life from me. Not telling me what she did when she snuck out of the house at night. How truly ironic it was, a vampire hunter's child being turned into the very monster they hunted. Breaking off those thoughts for now, I noticed that the sun was setting. Soon it would be nightfall. I was ready to prowl the night and break free from these castle walls. A few more minutes and I would be free. Anxiously I waited by the doors, the beast inside of me was awakening and howling. Eagerness crawled along my skin.

    When the sun had finally lay itself to rest, I burst through the castle doors. Being locked away in the castle all day felt clustered. I felt trapped like a beast in a cage. At night I was allowed to roam free. To run with the wolves and feast on the living. Donning a silk white dress my bare feet raced across the snow covered ground. On this very day, one hundred and fifty-five years ago it snowed. On this day, I murdered four hunters and turned one into my child. Into a child of night. My midnight hair whipped through the wind behind me as I bounded through the forest. This was my freedom. The night was mine to call my own. I was its ruler and it bowed down to me.

    The howling of wolves sounded in my ears. My body was eager to join them. They were hunters just like I. Wolves did not attack me, instead they welcomed me amongst them. Any animal of the hunt welcomed me like I was one of their own. Just like the previous night, I would run amongst them. I followed the sound of howls through the dark forest. But a scent wafted into my nostrils. A scent that forced my body to halt. Standing in the silence of the night my nose sniffed at the air around me. Blood. There was no mistaking that smell. It was not human blood that had been spilled but animal. More precisely, wolf. Changing direction, I followed the trail of the scent until I came upon a small clearing. And there, laid in the center of the clearing was the body of a wolf. Female. The moon's light shone down upon it. Crimson liquid painted the snowy ground around the creature. A pool of blood the body lay in. Kneeling beside the deceased wolf I noted that its belly had been gutted open and there laying in the creature's innards, was a young pup. It was barely breathing, struggling to hang on to the life that was slipping away from it. I could easily snap its neck and end its suffering but something inside of me told me this creature could live, if it were taken care of. My heart was not completely void of emotion. I felt love for creatures that reminded me of myself. Scooping the whimpering pup into my arms, I tore a long piece of fabric from my dress and wrapped it around the baby's shuddering body. Cradling the wolf to my chest I turned to leave but a familiar scent filled the air.

    My mouth formed into a smile as I turned around and peered up into the branches of a nearby tree. There, sitting upon the branch was the fiery haired woman I had turned one hundred and fifty-five years ago. Her appearance was exactly the same, though I knew it would not change. Vampires were ageless. Time could not touch our fair skin. My eyes caught the sight of a bloody dagger grasped within her hand. Anger flickered inside of me like a candle flame as I watched crimson droplets fall from the blade. She was the reason the wolf had died. Her face remained emotionless as she leapt down from the branch and approached me. "You were right, our paths would cross again."

    "And what is the meaning of your visit? Why did you return?"

    Her eyes glanced down at the pup held within my arms. "I wanted to test you."

    "For what, exactly?" My brow raised in question.

    Her now blue eyes did not move from the wolf. "To see if you were truly evil with no soul. No love for any living creature. I am glad you proved me wrong."

"Have you not noticed that you failed your own test?" My eyes glanced over her shoulder upon the dead wolf.

Meeting my gaze she said, "The wolf was already dead when I found it. I simply cut out the pup that was growing inside of it."

"I ask once more, why did you return?" My voice was demanding. It could bring out the truth in anyone, even vampires. All vampires except those of who ranked above me in royalty and years of living.

A sigh escaped her, "I am tired of denying what I truly am. It is time for me to give up the fantasy. Never again will I be human, never again will I be a hunter."

Her words were desperate and sad. Pitiful even. Many years she's lived denying to herself what she truly was. Feeling like an outcast amongst the living, fooling herself and those around her that she was human. Denying herself of the power and wisdom that we had. So many things I could teach her. I was ready to take her under my care. She was my child. Created by my doing and my blood. "Have you given yourself a new name? Or have you stayed with the one given to you at birth?"

Her eyes looked upon me with curiosity. "I can do that?" She reminded me of myself when I was first changed. Naïve and stupid.

"Yes, my daughter."

Laughter escaped me as her confusion and curiosity grew. "Why did you call me daughter? You are not the woman whom gave birth to me."

"You have much to learn. But first, choose a new name for yourself."

Her fiery brows knitted together as she thought deeply for a new name.

"Desdemona." She spoke after a few moments of thinking. Desdemona was an old name, much like mine and the queen's. I found older names to be more suiting for vampires anyhow. More elegant and fitting to our old nature and souls.

Nodding my head to her I said, "Desdemona is a suiting name for you."

Her arms crossed over her chest as her eyebrow raised. "Now, tell me why you called me daughter."

A sigh escaped me. Walking over to a fallen tree I seated myself upon it and called Desdemona over to sit with me. After she seated herself beside me I began to explain to her what she needed to know, for now. "You are my daughter. You were created from my bite. You are blood of my blood. The first of my bloodline. My child. I gave you the gift of eternal life."

"I've fed off humans, did I turn them when I bit them?"

"No. It requires more than just a bite to change a human into a vampire." The young wolf pup whimpered in my arms. It was freezing. Hungry.

"Then how do you change someone?"

Standing from the fallen tree I began to walk away from the clearing. The pup needed food and warmth or else it would die. "In time, I shall tell you all you need to know."

Speeding off into the forest, I searched for the pack of wolves. Hopefully, there would be a young mother amongst them that would be willing to feed the pup in my arms and take it into its care. It was far too young for me to take care of. Of course I will visit it, just like I do the pack of wolves. And maybe when its older I'll take it under my care. For now, though, it will remain with its own kin. Soon enough I was upon the pack. I spotted a young mother wolf feeding her pups, they had been alive only but an hour or so, I could tell. The mother did not snarl or growl at me, did not bite at me when I placed the young pup amongst the other feeding ones. Its tiny mouth clamped around a teat and it began to feed. I watched as it drank its fill of milk. The baby cuddled with the other pups and they drifted off to sleep with full bellies. My eyes made contact with the mother wolf. Her eyes were knowing.

Though a wild animal it may be, it understood me. She knew what I asked of her and she agreed. The wolf nodded her head to me and a smile crossed my lips. Wolves were intelligent creatures, that being why I admired them so. I knew the pup was in good care. It would grow up strong. Still my heart was saddened. My life was never ending while the wolf's life would come to an end eventually. My heart would grieve over its death, this I knew. Many animals I have owned as pets throughout the years I've been alive and many times I witnessed them pass from this world to the next.

"I thank you, young mother." Giving the pup one last pet I stood to leave.

Desdemona was leaned against the trunk of a tree, her eyes watching me carefully. As if she were studying me, determining if I truly had a heart or if it was dead like my soul. My heart was like ice when it came to many things. My love for animals however warmed it and the frost encasing my heart would melt away. Even in my human years I was weak when it came to animals, that was one of the few reasons why I enjoyed working on the farm.

"I've never met anyone quite like you." She spoke.

A chuckle left my lips, "Because Desdemona, there is no one like me."

"You are a complicated puzzle that I can't quite put together." Her brows knitted together.

Brushing past her as I began to walk away I said, "Come, it's feeding time."

We ran many miles searching through the forest for our meal. My nostrils caught the scent of two teenaged humans. A male and female. A laugh escaped me as I thought about what they could be doing. Soon enough we found ourselves at their campsite. The bonfire had died out, bright red embers and ash were all that remained of it as black smoke filtered into the night sky. Listening closely, I heard the sound of pleasurable moans coming from inside the tent. Many a time I have caught young lovers in the act. Back in my earlier years I would even join them, putting them under a trance and sucking the life away from them as we made love. Thrill crawled along my body as I waited to have my first drop of blood for the night. The ravenous beast inside me was awakening and craving the taste of the sweet nectar of life. Opening my mouth, I allowed my fangs to reveal themselves. My tongue slid across them. My finger nails grew long with sharpened points.

"How do you prefer your meal to feel when you are feeding? Terrified or unaware?" For me, the terror gave my body more of a thrill. It awakened a deep and dark entity inside of me. The beast. The demon. My craving intensified when the humans fought against me in my arms as they tried to flee. It only encouraged the beast inside of me. Though, when the human harbored a gentle and caring soul I preferred for them to be unaware. I preferred for them to live in hopes that they would make this world a better place. Unfortunately, once I started my feeding it was hard to stop. Resulting in the deaths of many innocents.

Desdemona approached me. Her crimson eyes glowing. "Terrified if they deserved to die. Unaware if they are innocents."

"Very well. Then these two shall live to see another day." Approaching the tent, I unzipped the flap and entered inside. The boy and girl were tangled in each other's limbs. Loud moans escaped their lips followed by heavy breathing. Love perspired in the air surrounding them. It was a sweet, delicate smell. Young love was a beautiful but tragic thing.

The boy's bright emerald eyes landed upon me and surprise filled his youthful face. I found myself getting lost in his colorful green gaze. For a human, he was rather handsome. His skin was perfectly tanned by the sun. Those dark locks of his were slicked back. His chin and jaw were chiseled and well defined. The girl also caught sight of me and a squeal of embarrassment and fear escaped her thin lips. Red and purple bruises blossomed on her neck and small breasts, those would prove to be hard to hide away from her parents.

My hands slid down my body, tugging at my dress. The silky

white fabric fell to my ankles in an ocean of fabric waves. I approached them closer, locking my eyes with theirs, forcing them under my trance. Their eyes grew wide with wonder. My body glided with seduction as I knelt before the young couple. My sharpened nails trailed down the young boy's muscular chest. I had to admit that his body was beautiful and well taken care of. He was entranced by my ageless beauty. A beauty that surpassed time. My finger placed itself underneath his chin and drew his face closer to mine. Delicately I planted a sweet kiss upon his lips. Deeper he fell into my trance. His lover did not protest my actions, for her eyes were only focused upon me.

    If a vampire was careful enough, we could kiss mortals without sucking the life from their lungs. But that took years of practice.

    The girl wondered how someone could be so beautiful, so perfect without flaw. Oh, if only she knew how flawed I truly was. If only she knew of the darkness that was my soul. Breaking away from the boy I moved on to the girl. Her face was round much like Selene's was. Youth spilled from her being. Her dark eyes peered upon me with curiosity. She sensed something was different about me but she could not figure out what exactly. There was a tinge of fear in the girl. That was expected. Leaning toward her, my hands grasped her face and I placed a careful kiss upon her lips. Now she too was lost in my trance. Feeding would soon begin. Calling out for Desdemona she soon joined me inside the tent. She picked her choice of meal, the girl. Desdemona's fangs sunk deep into the girl's neck once she brushed away the girl's dark brown hair. Blood cascaded down her tanned skin. The smell of it filled my nostrils, igniting my hunger. The girl let out a soft moan as Desdemona had her fill of the sweet, sweet liquid.

    The handsome boy was mine for the taking. His lower body was covered in the sleeping bag they had been making love in. My mind grew curious about what his lower portion looked like. My legs wrapped themselves around him as I pulled myself into his lap. My fingertips trailed across the softness of his cheek. My thumb traced over his bottom lip. It was so silky to the touch. I could feel the blood rushing through his veins like a river. His pulse beat beneath my fingertips crazily. His heartbeat pounded within my ears like drums. I would be lying if I said my body craved nothing more than just his blood. It had been several hundred years since a man made my body ache for pleasure. Already my mind was exploding in ecstasy and I had yet to drink his blood. Just the mere thought of our naked skins touching one another ignited the pleasure deep inside of me. Awakening a feeling and craving I had long since locked away.

 Those emerald eyes of his stared upon me with admiration. I wished for those eyes to never look away from me. His full attention was upon me. With my perfect, inhumanly sight I was able to count each one of his dark eyelashes. Noting the golden flecks that scattered throughout his irises like stars in a distant galaxy. It seemed as though, I myself, was falling into this human's trance.

 The boy's hands carefully trailed down my spine. His touch was gentle. His fingertips barely grazing my skin. Electricity seemed to ignite my skin wherever his hands touched me. Leaving behind a burning passion roaring through my body. I did not understand how a mere human could have this effect on my being. But I could not focus on that, I needed to feed. Leaning in closer to him, my lips brushed against the warm skin of his neck. My fangs pierced through it causing warm blood to pour into my mouth. A moan escaped him igniting my body at his pleasurable sound. Down the steamy, thick liquid cascaded in my throat. The beast inside me had awakened. It had its taste of the sweetest nectar and it wanted more. Too drain it from this boy's veins until his rivers of life ran dry. Though his blood was the sweetest I have ever tasted, I refused to drain him of life. I wanted him to live. Once I had my fill, I retracted my fangs and placed a tender kiss upon the mark I had left upon his perfect skin.

 Desdemona and I left the tent behind, left behind the lovers lost in their own wonderful worlds as they soared above the clouds. They were drifting away along the wind. Come tomorrow they would not remember a thing. They would wake with a terrible headache from the blood they had lost. But that was all and nothing more. After I had slipped on my dress Desdemona and I briskly walked through the forest, away from the campsite in case anyone was to come along and find the naked lovers. I noticed that my child kept questioning eyes upon me as we walked through the late winter's night. I waited for her questions that were sure to come. Approaching an old oak, I leapt into the air and landed upon one of its highest branches, seating myself upon it. The moon bathed my body in its glorious light. Desdemona joined beside me.

"Why did you not turn the human boy into a vampire?" That was a question I was not expecting.

My eyebrow raised, "Why would I turn him?"

"I saw the look in your eyes. The way you touched him and the way he touched you was as if you were lovers, or could be in this life." Very observant she was.

A sigh escaped my lips as I gazed up into the dark winter sky. "Many reasons prevented me from turning him."

"And the reasons being?" She was also very persistent as well.

"He already has a lover." Though, I had slept with married men in my earlier years it was not something I took pride in doing. I was naïve, rebellious I should say.

"Kill her." Desdemona surprised me speaking those words and with no emotion or care attached to them.

"This coming from someone who used to be a vampire hunter who swore to protect humans from monsters like us."

A mischievous smile crossed her lips. "That was another test and you passed. You would not kill her because in turn it would hurt the boy. This you know."

She read me like an open book. Saw through me like glass. In all my years of living no one has been able to do such. I had let my guard down around her without realizing it. This I never did around my kind or humans.

"If you do not trust me, then why test me?"

"Because, you are my creator. The only vampire I could come to trust. There are things I need to learn and you can teach them to me. After all, you are my mother and a mother teaches her children." Her now blue eyes watched my face closely, searching for emotion. "What is the other reason you refuse to turn him?"

"Because, I do not wish to turn him into a monster like us." My sharpened nails dug into the bark of the branch, splintering it.

A scoff escaped her lips, "Ha! You had no trouble turning me into a monster all those years ago. On this very day, I should say."

I had waited for her to make a remark such as that. "You are from my mother's bloodline. That was my reasoning for what I did to you." Meeting my gaze with hers I added, "I spared your life. You could have ended up like your friends." My voice was low and cold, it could strike fear into the bravest man.

She took no offense to what I had said, which surprised me. "You gave me a life I did not ask for."

"But you are glad you have it now, or am I wrong?"

Her eyes slipped away from my gaze and glanced at the night sky, she did not answer me. And she did not have too, for I already knew her answer. I watched her, studying her looks and comparing the similarities she shared with my mother. That fiery, wavy hair was a strong gene if it passed down through those generations and was gifted to this woman. In truth, I had always been jealous of my mother's hair. My father's genes decided most of my looks. His midnight hair and hazel eyes were given to me. When I was turned into a vampire I was saddened by the fact that I no longer had my father's eyes. They were one of the few things I inherited from that man. After I had been turned I did go and search for him and I found him. No, I did not speak with him because he had a new family and seemed happy. I was not angry with him for leaving and creating a new family, I was glad that he finally found happiness. Though he walked out on us, I still had love for him. I did not blame him for leaving mother, she was too far gone. Paranoia had taken control of her mind. Even I, her only child, walked out on her and left her all alone. Though she grieved over me she too, created a new family.

"What happens now?" Desdemona's subtle voice broke me from my thoughts.

Standing on the branch I leapt down from it and turned around to peer up at the woman. "Now, we return to the castle. It is almost sunrise."

Leaping from the tree, she landed beside me and together we began to walk away. "You trust me enough to take me back to the lair of vampires? Aren't you worried I might kill them all?"

My hand placed itself on her shoulder, "Oh, no I am not worried. For you see, they would kill you before you ever killed them. They are much older and stronger than you. I trust that you will not be that stupid to do something so foolish."

"Alright, you make a great point."

Dropping my hand from her shoulder I continued on walking ahead of her.

"Oh, and there's one thing I need you to do for me."

"And what would that be?"

Peering over my shoulder at her I said, "Reveal your fangs so your eyes will turn crimson. The queen must think that I have just turned you. Speak not of how old you truly are and what you used to be. Do I make myself clear?"

"Crystal." In a sarcastic filled move, she saluted me.

How interesting this would prove to be.

Castle of Vampires

Chapter Four

Returning to the castle, anxiety ate away at my being. It was true that I did not trust Desdemona, I would be foolish to do so, so easily. But, she was my responsibility now. And a mother takes care of her children. My eyes would be keeping a close watch on her. If she steps out of line once, then I will be the one to end her immortal life all too soon. Thus was also my responsibility. Throughout the years I have witnessed the queen murder her own children for various reasons. The way she killed them so quickly and easily without any emotion, was startling and terrifying. A dark shadow would cast itself over her face when she killed, especially if she had been betrayed. I learned at an early age to never betray the queen's trust for in doing so, it would end my life. My existence would be wiped away from the earth as if I were nothing to begin with. The queen radiated with a fierceness, a deadly aura, when she killed. In battle she was truly a frightening sight to behold but also beautiful. Her moves were intricate like a dance. She was a battle goddess many years ago. And since the wars have ended she no longer fights, leaving the battles to her children. More precisely, me. When the humans stopped bringing armies to our doorstep that's when the vampire hunters formed. A secret society of people who knew of our existence and wished to erase it from the face of the earth. They have been our enemies for several hundred years. Their only meaning in life was destroying us. Children of hunters were trained to be hunters as well, from an early age their days were spent training, making their human bodies stronger to fight against the immortal beasts that we were.

  My eyes glanced over at Desdemona. What was her life story? The night I turned her she did not seem too upset by the fact she was now the monster she once hunted. That very night she even killed her fellow comrades. Her actions made me question whenever she was truly satisfied with her life as a hunter. Was my decision what finally set her free from an unfulfilled life? My child did not seem to harbor any hatred toward me, if she did she was good at hiding it.

  Just as the sun was slowly rising, we entered into the lair of vampires. The men guarding the door regarded us with curious glances but said nothing. Nervousness radiated from Desdemona's being. I was very attuned to one's feelings. Their emotions vibrating from their being like ripples through the air around them. It was almost like reading a person's mind but also far from it. Worry did not consume me as we made our way through the castle, it was quite normal for a fledgling to be nervous so no one would think much of it. Questioning eyes rested upon us as we marched up the stairway and toward the queen's room. I had to inform her of my creation. Still worry was nowhere in sight, as long as Desdemona acted the part of a newly born vampire then everything will go smoothly. If not, then this would turn into a blood bath. For both of our sakes I hoped that would not happen.

  Lightly, my knuckles knocked upon the queen's door. As usual, I did not wait for her to answer and entered into her chamber with

Desdemona close behind me. The queen was laid upon her bed. Her naked limbs stretched out across the red satin bedding. She was truly a sight to behold. Her midnight locks had been braided together and snaked across the bed and onto the black marble flooring. Her dark brows rose with curiosity as she stood from her bed.

"My daughter, what have we here?" Her voice had a coolness to it that soothed your ears.

Taking a step forward I answered her, "The fledgling behind me is the first of my five children. She is blood of my blood." Glancing over my shoulder my eyes fell upon Desdemona, "She is my daughter."

The queen wrapped one of her pale arms around the cherry wood bedposts and rested her head against it. "After nine hundred and fifty-five years you have finally created another vampire. Tell me, what was so special about that human that made you decide to turn her into a creature of night?"

"I was going to feed from her but she reminded me much of my mother. They share the same color of fiery hair." That was no lie. Only a half spoken truth.

The queen regarded the girl behind me with questioning eyes. "What is this child's name?"

"Desdemona." I answered.

The queen nodded her head. She preferred the sound of olden names. Her arm slid down the bedpost as she made her way over to the woman. Desdemona grew worried but I gave her a glance that told her all was well. The queen had a very intimidating persona. Her body dripped with seduction but also radiated with strength. Within her gaze held hundreds, thousands of years of knowledge. The queen was wise and knowing. The most intelligent vampire to walk this earth. She has experienced history itself. Wars and plagues, she was there when it all occurred. Witnessing it for her own eyes. Beholding the tragedy that befell the human race. She circled around the woman, eyeing her closely. Examining her. Desdemona found herself face to face with the queen of vampires.

"Welcome young one, to the life of night. To the never ending cycle of living. Welcome to my family." The queen's dainty fingers reached toward Desdemona's fiery, wavy locks. She twirled a piece of her hair around her pale finger. "I shall have a room prepared for you."

Stepping toward the queen I said, "If it is no trouble, I wish for my child and I to share a room together."

Glancing over at me she took my suggestion into consideration. "It would be no trouble. I'll have a servant bring her up a bed and whatever else she may need."

"Thank you, mother."

"Anything for my first born." Her cold hand rested upon my cheek as a smile crossed her sweet lips.

Entering into my chamber, I found Selene setting up a bed for Desdemona in the sitting room. The couch had been moved to the adjacent wall to make room for the bed. Carefully she spread the satin sheet across the mattress and tucked the overhang underneath it. Once she had fixed up the bed she turned to leave and found Desdemona and I standing in the doorway. She was still as young and innocent looking as the day she was created. Her golden hair still styled into bouncy ringlets that brushed across her shoulders. No longer were her eyes the color of blood, now they were the same haunting blue as mine. They matched better with her innocent looks and nature. Her face was still round with youth since she was turned so young. Selene approached us with a sweet smile upon her bubblegum colored lips. "The bed is prepared for you, Desdemona."

News spread throughout the castle like wild fire so it did not surprise me that she already knew my daughter's name. "Thank you, Selene."

Fixing her round eyes on Desdemona once more she asked, "Is there anything else you may need?"

Desdemona's crimson eyes flickered over to me with a

questioning look upon her face. I nodded my head to her letting her know it was okay to speak. "No, thank you."

Selene nodded her head to us and left the room, quietly closing the door behind her on her way out. Desdemona approached her bed, her fingers trailed across the satin sheets. The color of her eyes shifted and returned to their once chilling blue hue. She lay her body to rest upon the mattress and stared blankly at the ceiling. Approaching my vanity, I slipped off my torn silk dress and tossed it upon the floor next to my cabinet of clothing. Seating myself upon the velvet cushioned wooden chair I grabbed a brush and set to work brushing the tangles from my long hair. As I worked the brush through my hair I found myself lost in memories from times past. Memories of my father. My earlier conversation with Desdemona caused the once vaulted memories to resurface. And I found myself reliving the day I had found my father with his new family.

Nearly a month has come and gone since my new life began as a vampire. Since my turning I have not paid my mother a visit and I never would for as long as she lived. I cared not about her. My heart held no love for that crazed woman. I was freed from her insanity and I could finally live my life. Now, I was on a search for the man who left us all those years ago. The man I once called father. Hate him, I did not. But love him, I did. My mother's constant paranoia drove him away from us. It was by her doing he left. That only fueled my resentment toward my mother.

Though I traveled through the night, the heat of summer was still unbearable. Sweat beaded down my brow as I bounded my way through the trees. My hair plastered to my forehead as I leapt from branch to branch. Soaring into the starry night sky. Wind whipped through my hair as I sped across the county side. The evening insects sang their songs, echoing throughout the air around me, filling my ears with their singing. Far off into the distance my eyes caught sight of a small cottage home. The glow from a candle's flame flickered behind a curtained window. My body grew anxious the closer the cottage home became. Soon I would find myself knocking upon the wooden door and facing the man that left me so long ago. Doubt clouded my mind as I closed in on the home. But the closer I came my ears began to hear conversations sounding from inside the house. Stopping just before a window, I peeped inside were a curtain was slightly opened.

What lay before my sight was a family sitting down for a late dinner. Happy smiles filled their faces as an older man spoke of a rather odd but silly thing that happened to him out on the farm. A young girl, seeming to be the age of four was seated next to the man. She resembled him. I noticed that her and I shared the same dark, thick hair. Even her eyes were the same as mine before the change. Her name was Alexandria which struck me as odd. Was my father trying to replace the child he had given up all those years ago? Did he regret leaving me behind in his past?

My eyes were still focused upon the young child. Though I hated to admit it, she was the most adorable child I had lay eyes on. I knew she would grow into a beautiful woman. So filled with youth and life she was. Her cheeks were bright like roses. Freckles scattered upon her pale skin like stars, forming their own little galaxy on the young girl. Then it dawned on me that the young girl was my half-sister. Watching my younger sibling saddened me deeply. Never would she know of the older sister she had. Never would I be able to meet her or play games with her on the farm. I began to think about all the memories we could have made together, all the laughter we could have shared. My hand came up to rest upon the cool glass of the window. Whatever was left of my heart slowly began to fade away. My emotions were a mixture of sadness, heartbreak, and abandonment. They swarmed around within my mind like a negative whirlwind. My hand clutched itself over my heart. Tears stung in my eyes as I watched my father's face glow with love and happiness. Never in my life had I witnessed my father's laughter. It was a deep sounding, joyful chuckle. Wrinkles formed *around his hazel eyes as his smile brightened.*

Mother and father argued so much that it was a rare sight to see my father smile but never had I seen him smile with such joyful happiness. When our small family was together, I was the only reason my father smiled. I was the only small happiness he had, but I wasn't enough to make him stay. He did not take me with him and I knew why. He wanted away from my mother, wanted to forget her. If he had taken me with him he would only be reminded of her whenever he looked upon me. My mother and I shared the same facial features, whether I liked to admit it or not it was true. This woman had ruined my human years, tore our family apart.

As I continued to gaze into the home the man's eyes slowly shifted over to the window I was staring in. Those hazel eyes of his locked with mine, surprise and realization flickered in them. His mouth seemed to form the name that I was once called by. The child beside him thought he was calling out her name, but he was calling out for me, the child he left behind. As he stood from the table I disappeared into the darkness of the night. Leaping into the highest branch of a nearby tree, I watched him emerge from the cottage home and enter into the night. Once more my name sounded from his lips as he called out. But his calls would be the only thing to answer him. I sensed a feeling of regret and sorrow seeping from his being. Regret for leaving me. Sorrow for not coming back for me. My father still loved me and still had love to give me but sadly I would no longer be in his life. Now, it was my turn to turn my back on him and leave.

As I began to leap to another tree he spoke out once more. One last desperate attempt in hopes I would return. "My dearest Alexandria, forgive me for the sadness I have caused you. You were my greatest happiness and I love you still." With a defeated heartbreaking look distorting his face, his shoulders slumped as he entered into his home. His final words to me would stay with me from now until the end of my days.

"And I love you, father." Those words whispered from my lips as

I leapt through the treetops with tears streaming down my cheeks like rivers.

Returning to reality I found that my memories still caused me pain. Tears burned within my eyes as I thought of the past. My fingers brushed against my wetted cheek. Upon my fingertips were the tears I had cried. Within my icy heart, I felt the same pain I had felt on that very day. I loved my father more than anything in this world. I could have turned him into a vampire. But I did not want to rip him away from his family and happiness. So many selfish things I had done throughout my long years but there was a time when selfishness had to be pushed aside so that others may be happy, even if it meant causing yourself a lifetime of grief. Unfortunately for me, this grief I would carry within my heart until the end of time. Humans were lucky in that way. Once their short lives were over no longer did they live with the ghosts from their past. No longer would they haunt them at night when all the world was quiet.

Peering into the mirror before me, I saw Desdemona's ghostly eyes staring back at me. "Did you grieve when your parents passed from this world?" I questioned her without breaking her gaze.

"Any child would grieve over their parents deaths."

Raising my eyebrow to her I asked, "But did *you*?"

A defeated sigh escaped her lips as her eyes shifted from my gaze. "My mother, yes. My father, well let's just say that on that evening I applauded the reaper of souls."

"You did not get along with your father?"

"He was a hunter and being my father, he was the one to train me. He wasn't very... *pleasant* with his lessons." A tinge of pain crossed her face. It almost seemed as though she winced.

Standing from the chair I approached the woman and seated myself next to her, "Tell me what he did." My voice drew forth her memories. Making her speak of her past life.

"Every day he forced me to train from dawn till dusk. If I even took a break he would whip me with a thin, bendable branch. Red, bleeding welts marked my back and legs. Scaring my skin. I was only ten years old. What does that say about a man who beats his child when her body couldn't handle the extensive training?"

"Any man that beats a child deserves the same punishment, times ten." I did not take kindly to men who beat their children. Once in my earlier years, I witnessed a father beating his young son without reason. The boy's nose had been broken and blood streamed from his nostrils. A fiery anger ignited inside my being. It didn't take me long to drain the life from his veins. The boy of course, ran away. Fleeing into his mother's arms. At least he no longer would face his father's wrath. Desdemona's father was a lucky man, he did not have to face the beast that I am.

"Did you grieve over your parents?" She turned the conversation away from herself. It was obvious she grew uncomfortable with having to speak of her past.

"You watched me moments ago grieving. The grief was over my father."

"What about your mother?"

"When my mother passed, I cared not." The day of her burial, I was there hiding in the shadows. She was only forty-five when her soul carried on to the other world. Her son, my half-brother attended the burial but much like I, he resented her. It vibrated off his being and rippled through the air. Her paranoia never left her and caused another one of her children to hate her.

"I don't understand why your mother never trained you to be a vampire hunter." Desdemona said.

"Maybe she didn't want me to become crazy like her." My voice grew cold as I spoke of my mother.

Desdemona's hand rested upon my shoulder causing me to stare into her blue eyes. "Or maybe she wanted to protect you from the monsters she faced."

Anger flickered inside of me as I listened to Desdemona trying to justify my mother's actions. But deep inside of me, I knew the words she spoke were true. My flame of anger was distinguished. "Maybe so." I had hated the woman who birthed me into this world, created me, and raised me. Looking upon Desdemona I wondered if she held any hatred toward me. My eyebrow raised as I questioned her, "Do you hate me?"

A bitter scoff escaped her lips as her hand fell from my shoulder, "I had hated you for nearly a hundred years for what you did to me on that night." Her face softened, "But hatred is not what I feel toward you now. I do not love you but I do not hate you."

"What has made you erase those negative feelings toward me?" In truth, I was surprised by her answer.

"Hatred is a tiring feeling to hold inside for years on end. It weighs down on your soul. I began to enjoy the new life I was given even though it went against everything I knew as a once hunter."

"You never wanted to be a hunter." Those truthful words formed on my lips.

A sigh escaped her, "No, I did not. Like I said, my father trained me to be one. Though my mother was strongly against it, he forced me into that life. I was never happy."

"Did you ever find a lover amongst the hunters?" The question was personal and a slight change of subject.

"No, I did not." Her eyes were watchful as they gazed upon me. "Did you ever have a lover?"

Memories flashed before my eyes and a saddened smile appeared on my lips. "Once. Long, long ago." The human boy we had found in the tent with his lover reminded me much of the man I loved many years ago.

"What was he like?" Desdemona grew curious. But I was not ready to tell her my life story.

"And that is tale for another time. For now, we rest." Standing from the mattress I walked over to my canopy bed. The wood was dark and rich. Red velvet curtains draped down from the tall posts and swept across the marble flooring. Pushing them back I climbed onto the plush mattress of my bed and wrapped my body in the silky crimson sheets. Vampires didn't need much sleep, a few hours was all we really needed. Though we could sleep for as long as we wished. We dreamed as well. But my dreams were never pleasant. Memories from my past haunted me in my sleep. The bodies of my victims would lay on the misty ground in pools of their own blood. Sometimes they would speak, shouting curses at me. I did not sleep for long.

Hypnotized by Beauty
Chapter Five

The following evening when the sun had finally set, I ventured from the castle into the cold winter's night. First, I would check to see how the young pup was fending. Second, I would feed. Though I didn't need the blood, I craved it constantly. It was a hunger that would never be filled. Traveling through the forest I kept high in the branches of trees to keep from being seen in case humans were camping or hunting near here. Soon I caught the scent of human, male, young. The scent was oddly familiar. I found myself where the young couple had camped. Standing in the middle of the small clearing, bathed in moonlight, was the handsome young man.

Hiding high up in the treetop my eyes watched the man closely. Even from this height I could count each one of his eyelashes, though I needn't have too because I had memorized the number. My memory was extensive, I remembered every moment of my long life. Even my first lover. The lover this human reminded me much of. The same dark hair, the same emerald eyes. Everything was hauntingly similar.

    The human man seemed to be searching for something. His eyes squinting into the dark forest. It was odd. What could he be searching for? Crouching low on the branch I continued to watch the human. I was fascinated by him. It still troubled me the way he was able to call the pleasure forth from deep inside my being. I remembered how sweet his blood was. The most savory blood I have ever drank. My tongue ran across my lips as my body craved the taste of him.

    The branch I had been sitting on snapped beneath me feet. Swiftly I landed on the heels of my feet on the snowy covered ground. The branch fell behind me. The human man quickly spun around, his emerald eyes taking me in with surprise and fascination. "It's you…" His sweet lips whispered into the night. His rich voice reverberated throughout my being.

    I did not answer him, only cocking my head to the side with confusion. He remembered me, but how? When I had finished drinking his blood I made sure he would never remember my face. Never remember what I had done to him. Now I was truly fascinated by him. A mere human. A human who drew forth my pleasure and has remembered me even after the trance I put him under. In truth, some part of me feared him.

    He approached me closer, "I came here to find you. To see if you were real."

    Instinct told me to run away. To leave and never look back. But I couldn't force myself to do so. I found myself trapped within his emerald eyes. "Why have you been seeking me?" My olden, wise voice startled him. For someone whom appeared so young it was indeed odd for such an older voice to speak from my lips. It marked the long life I have lived.

    "You are the girl that walked into my tent when I was with my girlfriend."

"And what makes you think that?"

"You are standing here right now. I know it's you." He took a step closer to me. "Since then I haven't been able to stop thinking about you."

"Now that you have found me, what do you plan on doing?" I strode across the snow covered ground toward the human man.

His emerald eyes seem hypnotized. In tranced by my beauty. "I-I don't know." He shook his head as a sigh escaped him.

"Tell me what brought you here tonight." My voice drew forth from him the truth. The reasoning behind his decision.

His tanned hand combed through his dark hair. He himself did not truly understand why he came here tonight seeking me out. "Mostly to see if you were real. I can't get you out of my head and it drives me crazy."

Spreading out my arms I said, "Here I stand. I am as real as the air you breathe." Now, it was time for me to leave this place. This human had a longing for me by my doing. He would go crazy searching for me, thinking of me. In order to break the curse, I have afflicted upon him, he needn't see me any longer. In time it would fade away much like his memory of me would. "Return to your lover and never seek me again."

Quickly he grasped my arm. A human never dared touch me in such a way. I should have struck fear into his very soul but fear is not what this human felt for me. He was brave and also naïve. "I can't go back to her." His voice was saddened.

"Turn your back to me and this place. Leave and never return. It is as simple as that." My voice grew cold with harshness. But I found that my heart ached at the thought of watching him leave.

As my eyes stared into his I could tell that he too was saddened by such a thought. "My girlfriend left me. I can't go back to her. And I can't stop thinking about you and the night in the tent."

It was too easy to trick a human into falling in love. But I had not played such a trick on this man. "What do you remember from that night?"

Without breaking his hold on me he said, "You came into the tent, undressed yourself, and crawled into my lap. You kissed me for a second. Then you bit my neck."

I shook my head and removed his hand from my arm. "You must leave this place. Don't come back. I am a monster and you'll only end up hurt in the end."

As I began to walk away from him he called out to me in a desperation. "Wait! There's something else!"

Stopping in my tracks I peered over my shoulder upon him. "What?"

"I-It feels like I've met you before. Before last night. I don't know, it's hard to explain." His words twisted in his mouth as he spoke, trying to voice his emotions and thoughts.

I was not sharing the same feeling as him. Because I knew we have never met before. I would have remembered such. The only thing that would make me think in such a way was the fact that he was similar to my first love. It was not possible for this human to stem from my lover's blood line. He was young like I and with no wife or children. So there is where his bloodline stopped, with him.

"I know you're a vampire." He spoke with confidence.

"Then you should fear me if you know what I truly am."

He advanced toward me, "I'm not afraid of you."

I took a step back from him. Why did I remain here playing this game with him? I should have left. I should have never came here. My own curiosity made me stay. This human was indeed fascinating and captured my interest. He had weaved his way into my frozen heart.

Revealing my fangs, I had hoped it would terrify him to see the monster that I truly am. But fear is not what I saw deep within his emerald gaze. Understanding seemed to shimmer in his eyes. This human was like no other. He was... *different.* The desire to turn him into a creature of night burned inside of me. But I did not wish to ruin his life and rip him away from his loved ones. He was young with so much life to live. I couldn't bear the thought of turning him. This life was not meant for him, not meant for someone so perfect. My first love died only after a few months of being a vampire. A damned hunter drove a stake through his heart. That hunter did not live to see another day.

"Please, leave." I pleaded to him. Something I never did was plead with helplessness sounding in my voice.

"I'll come back here, every night." His hand lightly touched my cheek sending a blazing fire coursing through my being.

"You are just a foolish human. All of you fall in love with beauty and you allow yourselves to be nothing more than dogs obsessed with perfection." My harsh words to him were meant to hurt him, to make him leave. But his eyes saw right through me.

"Promise me that you'll meet me here tomorrow."

"I cannot promise you that." I stepped away from him, away from his gentle touch. My body began to melt away into the darkness of the night. Disappearing from human sight. The human called out for me and raced toward the trees I had hidden behind. But I was no longer there. High in the treetop I watched him and listened as he called for me with desperation in his voice. Then, with a defeated sigh, his shoulders slumped and he turned his back to me. He too, faded away into the darkness of the night.

Once I could no longer hear the sound of the young man's heartbeat, I bounded through the forest in search of the wolves. My mind would not rest until I saw the young pup. Though I knew it wouldn't have changed much since the night before, I wanted to see if the mother wolf had taken care of it. To see if it survived the harsh winter's night.

Perching on a tree branch my eyes gazed down at the wolves below me. The mother wolf was feeding her young pups and the one I had brought to her. It seemed to be fending well. A hint of pride burned within my chest. Wolves were strong animals. The pup would grow up well. A smile tugged at my lips. I wished to hold the wee pup within my arms but I didn't wish to disturb it. Sleep soon fell upon the tiny creature. A small, adorable yawn escaped him and soon his eyes closed and he drifted off into the land of dreams.

My craving for blood resurfaced. I still needed to feed. Leaping down from the branch my feet landed silently upon the ground. Bounding through the dark forest I was in search of another human to feast on. My ears rang with the sound of chatter. Two older men. My nose caught their scent and I followed the trail of it. My eyes caught sight of them. They were seated upon a fallen tree before a fire. Their shotguns resting beside them. I caught the scent of blood. Wolf. Searching around their campsite my eyes landed upon the corpses of two wolves. The top of the creature's heads was nearly gone. A bullet wound. Anger blazed through my veins like a crazed fire. Within my mind I planned how they would die. One of them I would rip their throat out, the other I would shoot with their own gun. The one who fired the deadly weapon upon nature's creatures. The beast inside me had awakened.

Hiding my body behind the trees, I found myself standing directly behind the men. I would save the shooter for last. For now, I would make him fear what I am. Leaping from behind a tree I grabbed the first man. Wrapping my arms around his waist I drug him back into the dark forest. He screamed loudly. Cursing me. Trying to break free of my grasp. A bitter laugh escaped me. Did he not know that he was only fueling my craving? The beast? Of course he did not. The man's heartbeat pounded within my ears. It was beating fast out of terror. Fear gripped his soul. He knew he was going to die. There was no escaping. The man's life has come to an end. He began to plead for his life, begging me to spare him. Leaning down to the man's face I planted a soft kiss upon his lips and whispered into his ear, "You have met your end."

The man's eyes almost bulged from their sockets as he watched my finger nails grow long and sharp. A smirk wrote itself upon my lips as my nails sunk into the man's neck. Slowly. The warmness of his blood caressed my skin, igniting my thirst. The man lay there choking on his own blood. It poured from the corners of his mouth and dripped onto the snow blanketed ground. My tongue licked at the escaping blood. It burned in my mouth. The beast inside me was howling because it finally had its taste of blood, and wanted more. This man's blood had to wait. There was one human left that needed to be dealt with.

As I stepped forth from the shadows the other man quickly grabbed his gun and aimed it at me. I stared down the double barrels of the shot gun. A chuckle escaped me. My eyes could see the man's hands trembling. Sweat began to bead down his brow. His finger pulled the trigger. *Pow.* My eyes watched the bullets cut through the air toward me. Everything slowed down, except me. My hands reached out and grabbed the bullets within my palms. They were hot and burned my flesh. The man's eyes met with mine. Terror built up inside of him. Tossing the gun to the ground he tried to flee but he didn't get very far. In a blur I rushed toward him. My finger nails dug into his shoulder blades and flung his body to the ground. Snow flew into the air around him as he fell. The man was in too much pain to move. He would not be fleeing again. Waltzing over to the fallen tree, I grabbed the other gun. The muzzle of the gun dragged along the snowy ground behind me, creating a thin trail. Approaching the man, I aimed the muzzle of the gun to his head. Tears brimmed in the man's brown eyes. Laughter escaped me.

"P-Please… spare me!" He bellowed loudly.

I shook my head slowly. "I cannot."

"What have I done to you! Why are you doing this!" Tears streamed down his face. A wet spot formed in the crouch of his jeans. He had wetted himself out of fear. Pathetic human.

"The wolves you murdered did no harm to you or anyone else." My voice was cold as ice.

"Hunting is a sport! They are just animals!"

"Tsk. Tsk. You hunt for sport. I hunt for *blood*."

My finger hooked around the trigger. Then, the sound of a gun rang off into the distance on this cold winter's night. The man's head had been blown open. It was truly a gruesome sight to behold. But it did not sicken me. During my long life I have witnessed things much worse than this. I slung both straps of each gun over my shoulder and approached the men I had killed. Grabbing them by their ankles I began to drag them back to the castle of vampires. Feeding time would soon begin.

Returning to the castle, I dumped the lifeless corpses upon the floor in the feeding room. Blood splattered across the floor. Hisses and snarls sounded from behind the door. The criminals were hungry. A servant entered into the room and asked if she should inform the queen of the bodies. Once I had nodded my head to her she rushed from the room to find the queen. Leaving the room, I closed the door behind me and ascended up the stairs. Upon entering into my room, I found Desdemona and Selene conversing with one another. Desdemona did good in remembering to keep her fangs revealed so that her eyes appeared crimson. No one would question why her fangs were out, fledgling vampires found it hard to control their new bodies. Their newly found strength, hearing, sight, and fangs. We need only to keep this charade going for a few more days.

Selene's round blue eyes landed upon me, "Good evening, Princess Nehemiah. How was your night?"

Servants were rarely allowed to leave the castle. Each evening when I left and returned Selene would ask me the same question. "Two humans made the mistake of murdering my favorite animal. Needless to say, they no longer breathe on this earth."

"Did you bring their bodies to the feeding room?" Selene asked.

"Yes. You and the other servants will feast well tonight."

Servants never fed with royals. They had their own separate nights of feasting.

Her blue eyes glistened with happiness. She knew that whenever I brought them humans, I always brought more than one. Other royals treated the servants like animals and would only bring them one human. Tonight, the servants would feast well.

"Thank you!" Selene threw her arms around me and wrapped me in an embrace. She still acted like the young sixteen-year old she once was. Something I admired about her, she was able to keep her sweetness and innocence even after being turned into a monster. Selene was one of the few people I allowed to touch me in such a way.

Returning the embrace I said, "You're more than welcome."

Selene rushed from the room, ready to feast and quench her thirst. Approaching my wardrobe, I swung open the massive doors and began to search for my favorite evening gown. My hands searched through dresses that were hung upon the metal rod. Soon, I found the pearly white, floor-length dress. It was crafted from sheer fabric. It would indeed expose my body but that was something I no longer cared about. Slipping off my pants and shirt, I slid the silky fabric down my body. It caressed my skin lovingly. There were no sleeves to the dress, only thick straps that clung to my shoulders. The neck of it cut into a low V down between my breasts. The skirt of the dress swept across the dark flooring in pearly white waves. Approaching my vanity, I seated myself upon the chair and set to work weaving my long hair into a braid.

Desdemona's crimson eyes watched me in the mirror's reflection. "I followed you tonight." She spoke.

Continuing my braiding I said, "I know."

She blinked at me, "How?"

My eyes matched with hers, "You forget that I am older and wiser than you, young one. Now, tell me why you followed me."

"To see what you would do."

I raised my brow in question to her, "Testing me again?"

Desdemona broke her gaze away from mine, "You are a

complicated being. You have love for animals, that was made obvious tonight when you murdered those humans without thought. You kill without reason."

My brush cracked against my wooden vanity as I rose from my chair. Her words angered me. "I have reasons for killing." I approached her. Anger fumed from my being. "Your friends wished to kill me and the other vampires within this castle. That was my reason. Those humans killed wolves who had done no harm to anyone. That was my reason." Lowering my head, I matched my gaze with hers. "Do not dare judge my actions. You are not innocent yourself. Your hands are covered in blood just like mine." My voice grew cold as harsh words escaped my lips. Desdemona grew nervous and coward under my strong gaze. I knew I sent a chill of fear down her spine. She would do well to keep her thoughts to herself.

Returning to my vanity, I finished braiding my hair and tied it off at the end. "What else did you witness tonight?" I questioned her.

Her voice was quiet. "You spoke with the human boy."

"I did."

"Why do you refuse to turn him?"

A sigh escaped me, "I have told you my reasons."

She stood from her bed and approached me. "I know. But I feel as though there is one more reason you have not told me."

"When I created you, you were born of my blood. You are now my daughter." My eyes met with hers, "Do you see where I am going with this?"

"It would make him your son."

I nodded my head to her. "Then it would be taboo for me to love him and for him to love me. It would be incestuous." My skin crawled at the thought.

"Would it not be considered taboo for a vampire to love a human?" She said.

"I do not love the man."

"But you will, slowly." The words Desdemona spoke, would

prove to be true. "I can change him for you."

Rising from my chair I shook my head. "No. I won't allow him to be turned into a monster."

As I was pulling back the curtains from my bed Desdemona said, "You call us monsters. Even yourself. Do you truly believe that we are all monsters? That there is no light inside of us or hope?"

A saddened sigh escaped my lips, "There is no light for those who live in the dark."

Creatures of the Night
Chapter Six

The following evening, I brought Desdemona along with me. It was too risky leaving her alone, it could expose that she is no fledgling. Expose that she is older than she seems. That she was once a hunter of our kind. The queen would not take too kindly to that. She would strike Desdemona down before me. Or force me to do it instead. What would the queen do with me? I feared the answer to that. The queen was the one person I truly feared on this earth and the one person I admired most.

"Are we meeting the human?" She questioned.

Before I had realized it, we found ourselves at the clearing. Something drew me here, pulled my body to this location. "We must leave before he arrives." Before I could leave Desdemona reached her arm out and grasped my forearm. Her finger nails dug into my skin.

"Release me, now." My voice commanded her.

She struggled to fight against my command but still she held me. "You were drawn here for a reason, Nehemiah. Stay and see why."

Before I could answer her, the sound of footsteps approached. The beating of a familiar heart rang in my ears. The smell of male human wafted into my nostrils. My eyes watched as he stepped forth from the darkness of the forest. His emerald eyes shone in the moon light. I could see the golden flecks that scattered throughout his irises. My heart leapt at the sight of him. His dark hair had been slicked back. His lips twitched into a smile at the sight of me. Those emerald eyes of his took me in. "I had a feeling you would show up." His rich voice spoke to me.

"We were just leaving. You should do the same." As I turned around I found Desdemona blocking my path. Her eyes were stern. "Move."

"No. Speak with him. Find out why you were drawn here."

A defeated sigh escaped me as I turned around to face the human. "Why did you wish to meet again?"

He approached me, "I wanted to see you again. And I never caught your name."

"Nehemiah. What is your name?"

"Your name is different, haven't met anyone with that name before. Mine is Emrik." A strangely odd name for a human. A name that is very old. Perhaps he was named after a great-grandfather? The name suited him.

"Emrik, return to your life. Leave here and never look back." My voice was soothing as it whispered from my lips. I tried to persuade him into leaving, but he did not move. He was not put under my trance like other humans.

His face grew saddened. "I don't have much of a life to return to. Coming here is my only escape."

My head cocked to the side, "What are you escaping from?"

A sigh escaped him as he seated himself upon a fallen tree.

Desdemona nudged my back, urging me to sit with him. Shooting her a warning look I walked over to the human and seated myself beside him, but not too close. His blood roared through his veins. The beast inside of me heard it and wanted a taste. I resisted the urge to feed. No longer would I drink this man's blood. This thought saddened me, and also made me realize how monstrous I truly was. Not being able to taste his sweet, sweet blood again. Oh, how the beast inside of me did not like that. It howled louder and clawed at my soul as I listened to the man's heart beat. It was much like a song to my ears, music that I could listen to forever.

Emrik's jaw clenched and his brows knitted together. "I'm escaping from my father." Anger and fear radiated from his being and rippled through the air around us. The smell of fear plagued my nostrils.

"Why?"

His hands balled into fists, the veins in them rising to the surface of his skin. "He's an alcoholic. When he drinks he..." He bit his bottom lip and shook his head.

My hand delicately rested upon his shoulder and my head tilted over to peer into his emerald eyes. Sadness could be found within his gaze. "What does he do?" My voice urged him to continue.

"When he's drank too much he turns into another person. When I was younger he used to beat me until I stood up to him and broke his nose. But now, he hits my mom." He gazed into my eyes. "I try to stop him but he beats her when I'm not around to protect her."

Anger flared inside my being. Abusers deserved a punishment that was far worse than any beating they dealt out. "Why don't you and your mother leave him?"

A helpless sigh escaped him, "We don't have the money to live on our own. My dad is a wealthy business man but my mother is out of work."

There was something I could do to help them. No, I would not kill his father, though the thought of it pleased me. Instead, I would simply visit the man and very *kindly* ask of him to give them enough money to live on their own. If he refuses, then it'll be a fun evening for me. "Do not worry, Emrik. All will be well."

A scoff escaped him, "I wish I could believe that."

I forced him to meet with my gaze. "Believe in me."

The look within his eyes seemed hopeful, like for just a moment he believed in me. "I wish I could, Nehemiah."

A fiery warmth blazed throughout my being when his lips spoke my name. "You can, Emrik. I am capable of many things."

His hand rested atop of mine. His warmth caressed my skin. I could feel the blood rushing through his veins. "That, I believe. But my family problems are not anything for you to worry about."

"I can help you, if you allow me to do so." My voice spoke to him.

Before he could answer me a loud, continual ringing sounded from his jean pocket. His hand dug into it and retrieved a phone. His finger touched the screen and he held it up to his ear, "Yeah?"

An older man sounded from the phone, his words were slurred. Obviously drunk. "Emrik, where the hell are you? Get your ass home, now!" Then the phone went silent when the man ended the call. A distressed sigh escaped Emrik's perfect lips.

"I have to go." He turned to face me, "Meet me again tomorrow?"

I shook my head. "No. Your father is angry that you are out this late at night. His abuse is not worth sneaking out here." As I stood from the tree he reached out and grasped my hand.

Staring into his eyes, they pleaded to me with such sadness. Such helplessness. "Please, you're the only thing that distracts me from the hell I live in."

"Emrik, you don't know me. You don't know how dangerous I am or how dangerous it is to be around me. Return to your human life, make normal friends. Concern yourself with me no longer." As these words spoke from my lips a tiny crack would form in my frozen heart.

He stood from the tree, still holding tightly onto my hand. He towered over me. "Nehemiah, please. My *human* life is dangerous living with my father. Can we continue to meet every night? It's the only thing I have to look forward too."

My feelings were conflicted. I knew continuing to meet with him was dangerous. His life would be put in danger if the queen were to find out about our meetings. But as I looked into his eyes, deep within my heart I wanted to see him again. So much of him reminded me of my first lover. It was hard for me to resist this human. "Alright." I finally said.

A broad smile spread across his lips. His eyes lit up with happiness. "See you tomorrow." Emrik said.

"Tomorrow." The human rushed off, disappearing into the forest. Away from my sight. Desdemona approached me and stood by my side. "I did not find out why I was drawn here."

Her hand rested upon my shoulder, "You did. The boy needs help. Your help."

"Creatures of night do not meddle in the lives of those who live in light."

"You'll meddle in this human's life."

A stern look crossed my face as I raised an eyebrow to Desdemona, "And what makes you think that?"

She crossed her arms over her plump chest, "I saw your face when he spoke of his father. You were already planning something for the man. I saw it within your eyes."

A sigh escaped me as I broke my gaze away from hers and peered off into the dark forest. "I wish you wouldn't read me so easily."

"Part of my training as a hunter was to learn my opponent's facial and bodily expressions and movements so I could determine their next attack."

"You know, I've always admired how much you hunters trained. Just mere humans but some of you are able to hold a fight against vampires. That alone is admirable." I admitted.

A smile twitched at the corners of Desdemona's lips. A hint of pride blazed through her. "My father never told me he was proud of me or even acknowledged how much effort I put into my training." A sarcastic chuckle escaped her, "But I am hearing praise from a creature I trained to kill."

"Better to hear it from someone than no one. No matter what human or *creature* it comes from." I said.

"Thank you, Nehemiah."

With that, we returned to the castle. The sun was rising. We did not feed. I had wasted precious time speaking with the human. But I had a feeling brewing inside of me that there would be a feast. The beast inside me craved the taste of blood.

Upon returning to the castle, I ascended up the stairs and traveled to the queen's room. Desdemona was close on my heels behind me. When we approached closer to the queen's chamber the sound of fearful sobbing rang in my ears. Opening the door my eyes caught sight of a servant girl kneeling before the queen. Her body trembled and reeked of fear. My nostrils flared at the disgusting scent. She sobbed loudly. The room echoing around us with her cries. The queen stared upon the girl with emotionless eyes. She hated weakness. Weak ones did not survive long. The queen's blue eyes faded into crimson. Her fangs revealed themselves. She strutted around the weeping girl. Her midnight locks trailing across the floor behind her. Slowly she circled the servant. Disgust radiated off the queen's being. The fledgling servant had done something to anger the queen but what she did, I did not know.

"Please my queen. Forgive me." The girl's crimson eyes stared upon the queen. Tears stained her face. How truly pathetic she appeared.

"You fed from the royal's humans for the feast. A servant should know better than to do so. How truly ignorant you have proven to be." The queen's lips pulled back in a snarl.

"I-I'm sorry! I was so hungry! The blood smelled so good..." The girl's hands clutched the hem of her dress. Her head tilted down to the ground, breaking away from the queen's chilling gaze.

The queen knelt before the girl, her fingers hooked underneath the servant's chin forcing the girl to meet with her gaze. "Feeding without thought is reckless." Slowly, the queen's finger nails grew long and sharp. Sinking into the girl's chin. Blood cascaded down the queen's fingers, dripping onto the floor. The servant's eyes grew wide with fear. Once more she pleaded but the queen ignored the girl's cries. Removing her claws from the girl's chin she sunk her hand into the girl's chest. Crimson gushed from the massive wound. When the queen removed her hand within her grasp she held the girl's heart. An empty cavity was all that remained. The servant's eyes rolled into the back of her head and her body toppled over onto the ground. Blood poured around the body creating a pool of crimson. The queen crushed the heart she held between her fingers and tossed it next to the corpse. It made a disgusting sound as it splattered across the floor.

    Behind me, Desdemona's aura rippled with fear and anger. Her body trembled. This was the first time she witnessed the queen's cruelty. Something she would grow used to seeing. The queen gazed upon the corpse with disgust and shook her head. "Fledglings are truly naïve. Ignorant. Feeding without thought. Breaking my rules." The queen's eyes narrowed as she peered at Desdemona. "Let this be a lesson to you, young one. Never go against my word."

    Turning her attention to me she said, "Nehemiah fetch a servant to remove this *filth* from my sight." With that the queen entered into her bathing chamber and closed the door behind her.

    Leaving the queen's room, I informed a servant to clean the mess and to do so without question. Unfortunately, the servant girl was close friends to the one the queen had killed. As she removed the body she cried quietly to herself. Desdemona did not utter a single word as we made our way toward my room. She was distraught after having to witness the queen murder a servant. Even I had to admit that it was unnecessary for the queen to kill the young fledgling in such a way. It was gruesome, really. Still, I have witnessed the queen do much worse than that. So I did not dwell on this for long. Though Desdemona, on the other hand, would.

Entering into my chamber, Desdemona began to speak her mind on the event that occurred before her eyes. "She shouldn't be allowed to do such things! The servant said she was hungry, why does it matter if she fed from the royal's feast? She was a vampire just like us!" Anger flared throughout her being.

"The queen's word is law. If we do not abide by her rules, then we are punished."

"You can't tell me that you think it is right for her to do that."

Brushing past her I said, "There is no true right, Desdemona."

She tried to argue more on the subject but I dismissed her words and climbed into my bed, closing the drapes, shutting me away from Desdemona. Soon she would learn what it truly means to be a vampire. Soon she would learn to abide by the queen's word without thought. If not, then she too would end up like that heartless servant.

Desdemona stood behind the curtains of my bed. A lit candle behind her cast her silhouette upon the drapes. "Does it goes against the queen's word to love a human?"

I did not respond to her question, for she already knew the answer. Turning my back to her I drifted off to sleep. My dreams were not haunted by my past victims. Instead my mind was plagued by Emrik. The heartbreakingly beautiful human.

Paying a Visit
Chapter Seven

When night fell across the land I headed out into the human world.

There was something I must do. Someone I must see. Tonight I would be paying a kindly visit to Emrik's father. Depending on how he responds to my offer, he might just live to see another day. Or he might not. Though the thought of killing him pleased me, I knew that it would hurt Emrik. Even though the man was an abusive alcoholic, the boy still had love for his father.

    Making my way through the forest I found myself coming upon a gravel road. Humans chopped down trees to create this so that they may travel through here with ease. Selfish acts done by a selfish race. They had no love for nature. Only destruction. One day maybe nature will pay the humans for the karma they deserved for hunting innocent animals and destroying forests.

Racing along the gravel road I followed the scent of Emrik. His trail was still fresh. The cold weather allowed for his scent to remain longer. Frozen within the air. Emrik's scent seemed to be closer than I thought. Like he lived somewhere in these deep woods. Soon enough I found myself standing in the backyard of a cabin home. Black smoke filtered into the night sky from the chimney. Someone was inside. It was not Emrik. His heartbeat was nowhere to be found. Instead what my ears heard was the sound of arguing. Approaching the cabin home closer I peered inside the window. An older man and woman stood in kitchen. The man held a can of beer within his grasp. His dark hair was a mess, his tie undone and his white collared shirt was unbuttoned, exposing his gut. The woman that stood before him was crying. Her cheeks were flushed. It was made obvious that she feared this man. He continued to yell at her. She shook her head to his angry question. The can of beer exploded across a kitchen wall, drenching it in alcohol. The man's hand slapped the woman across her crying face and down she fell onto the cold tile floor.

Anger flared inside my being as my eyes watched the woman plummet to the floor. No longer would I stand idly by. It was time to pay the man a visit. My fist crashed through the glass of the window, startling the married couple. As I climbed inside the man began to yell at me. His mistake.

"Who the hell are you? Get out of my house!" He approached me with a fist raised. "Look at what you've done!"

As his fist slowly came towards me I caught it in my grasp. My finger nails grew long. "I don't take kindly to men who abuse." My voice was cold and harsh. His gaze wavered as I stared deeply into his eyes.

"Mind your own business, bitch!" His breath reeked with alcohol. He had drunk more than just a few beers.

Slowly twisting his wrist he winced in pain. I stopped it just before his bone snapped. "I cannot help but intervene when I see someone abusing a woman or child. And you, have done both."

"I-I haven't abused a child!" He bellowed loudly.

Shaking my head I said, "Ah, but you have."

"You don't know anything about me! All of that is a lie!" His continual yelling began to hurt my ears.

Forcing his back against the kitchen wall, my hand found itself around the man's neck. I could feel his blood roaring through his veins beneath my fingertips. "I do not speak of lies. I have witnessed the pain you caused this woman." My voice remained calmed.

The man glanced over at the woman on the floor. "Mary, call the cops! Get this bitch arrested!"

My grip tightened around his throat and lifted his body into the air. His feet dangled. "She will not be calling anyone." Peering over my shoulder I said, "Isn't that right, Mary?" Putting her under my trance, she slowly nodded her head. My soothing voice convinced her, hypnotized her.

Peering into the man's eyes I said in a low voice, "Now, you will leave. You will never come back to this home and harm this woman and her child again."

"You can't make me leave! This is my house and my wife!"

My finger nails pierced his skin. "You *will* leave or you'll have to face the monster I am." Slowly, my fangs began to reveal themselves. My eyes turned crimson. Fear began to perspire from his body. He trembled within my grasp.

"Now, I will give you the chance to leave. But if you ever return here and harm these people, I will know. And I won't hesitate to kill you."

Dropping the man back on his feet, I backed away and crossed my arms over my chest. "I will give you till the count of three."

"That's not enough time for me to get my shit together!"

"Isn't that a shame? One." I began my count.

The man quickly snatched the car keys from the kitchen counter and made his way out the back door. The sound of an engine starting roared into the night. Tires sounded across gravel road and the car slowly disappeared off into the distance as the man drove away. And hopefully would never return.

The woman named Mary finally stood from the floor. She seemed shaken, which was understandable. "Are you alright?" I asked.

"Y-Yes. Who are you?" Her emerald eyes stared upon me with curiosity. She did not fear me.

"I am no one." I turned my back to her and leapt through the broken window. "Your husband's wallet is on the counter. He should have plenty of money in his bank account for you to live on." I shouted as I disappeared into the night.

Emrik stood in the clearing. His emerald eyes searched for me through the darkness. He wondered where I was. For a moment, I thought about leaving and not meeting him. He would be safer if we were to never see one another again. But once again I felt myself being drawn to him. My body being pulled to him. My soul seeking him. Leaping down from a tree branch, I landed a few feet behind him. Startled he quickly turned around. Our eyes met. I grew hypnotized in those emerald eyes of his. Such a beautiful green they were. The golden flecks scattering throughout his irises appeared like a galaxy. I could tell that he too, was being drawn to me. Like our souls have been searching for each other.

For a moment I thought my first love had returned to me. That he had come back from the other world and searched for me. Breaking the laws of life and death to return to this world. My mind wondered off into distant memories of my past. Memories of my lover.

A gentle breeze brushed past. My long dark hair sailed across the wind. The warmness of the day was settling down as night was being called forth. The sky began to grow ever darker as the moon rose into the sky, claiming the night as its kingdom. When the moon ruled over the sky, that is when creatures of night came out to play.

    Sitting upon a cliff that overlooked the sea, my love approached me. His clear blue eyes stared into mine. Forever I could gaze into them. Warmth blossomed within my heart as he pulled my body into his lap. His strong arms encircled my waist, his fingers trailed down my spine lovingly. His dark locks curled around the sides of his face, some of them falling into his ever clear eyes. A smile tugged at the corners of his perfect lips. His pearly white teeth shone in the moon's light.

    "What mischief do you have planned for tonight, love?" His rich voice spoke to me.

    "Hmmm. I am rather thirsty. Perhaps we could feed?"

    His lips trailed along the skin of my neck. "We could. Or we could do something else more pleasing." His teeth nipped my skin. Pleasure rose into my being.

    "Feeling playful tonight, my love?" I whispered into his ear.

    "Perhaps. Tonight I wish to spend with my woman. Tomorrow we can feed." His eyes met with mine.

    "Tonight love, tomorrow blood." I placed a sweet kiss upon his soft lips.

    Laying my body upon the ground gently, he climbed on top of me. His eyes stared endearingly into mine. My heart began to race. It beat crazily within my chest. Nathaniel's heart went wild as well, it drummed in my ears. Love perspired from our bodies and filtered into the air around us, swirling around our beings. Such a sweet and delicate scent it was. A rose is what it smelt like with a hint of honey. It was a scent I would remember for years to come.

    My hands placed themselves on either side of Nathaniel's face. "I love you." Those sweet words whispered softly from my lips.

    "And I love you." His words were much sweeter to hear. They warmed my heart and made it flutter within my chest. My being was enveloped with happiness.

    "Forever?" I questioned.

    "Forever." He answered with a kiss.

Only our little forever did not last as long as we had wished. A few years later Nathaniel was killed at the hands of a hunter. My love was taken from me on that day and so was heart. Since then, the beast inside of me truly awakened into the blood thirsty, murderous creature it was.

Emrik still stood before me. Though it felt like I had been lost inside my memories for hours, it had only been a few seconds. My heart ached as my eyes stared upon the human before me. So similar they were. Almost like this human was put onto this earth to torture me. Remind me of my lost love.

"I was beginning to think you wouldn't show." He finally spoke in that voice that sounded so familiar.

"I should not have come."

Stepping toward me he said, "You say that, yet you are here."

"You aren't safe around me. Why won't you leave me alone?"

"I can't stop thinking about you. I even dream about you." Was my trance a lingering effect? Was he still under its influence? But it has been days since that night in the tent. It couldn't still be effecting him.

Gazing down at the ground I whispered a question, "What do you dream about?"

Peering back at him I saw his cheeks flushed. Embarrassment rippled off his being. His hand brushed through his dark, shaggy locks. "You'd laugh if I told you."

"I would not."

A sigh escaped him, "Last night I dreamt that we were on a beach."

"What were we doing on the beach?"

"You loved the ocean and wanted to see it, so I took you there."

His dream reminded me of time when Nathaniel surprised me. He had carried me all the way to the beach. Though it wasn't much of a surprise. Vampires have a good sense of hearing and smell. I remembered the first time I heard the waves of the ocean gently crash onto the sandy shore. I remembered the salty smell in the air. Those things I would never forget in my long years.

"You didn't answer my question."

Once more his cheeks flushed. "We were... making love." He admitted embarrassed.

"Ah, I see."

Part of me was jealous that he had such a dream. My dreams only pictured Emrik's face. The sound of his voice would echo around my mind, whispering like a whirlwind. He had replaced my victims, no longer did I see their faces. No longer did I hear their cries of sorrow.

"I better go, my dad will get mad again." Emrik said.

As he began to walk away I reached out and grasped his arm. His emerald eyes met with mine. "You needn't worry about him anymore."

His dark brow raised in question. "What did you do?"

Releasing my hold on him I said, "I didn't kill him if that's what you're worried about."

"That doesn't tell me what you did." His muscular arms crossed over his chest.

"You wanted you and your mother to live on your own away from him. I made that possible. He won't be living with you anymore."

His eyes widened with disbelief. "How did you do it?"

"You forget what I am. It wasn't too hard to convince him to leave."

"I-I don't know what to say." His words fumbled from his lips.

My hand rested gently upon his shoulder. "You don't have to say anything."

His eyes met with mine once more. "Thank you, Nehemiah."

Stepping away from him I said, "Return home. I'm sure your mother would like to see you."

"Tomorrow night will I see you?"

"Perhaps, perhaps not."

With those parting words I disappeared into the night. And I could have sworn I heard Emrik chuckle. A smile spread across my lips. Of course I would see him tomorrow. And he knew that.

Returning to the castle and my chamber, Desdemona looked upon me with questioning crimson eyes. Her fiery eyebrow raised. "I smell the human all over you. You met with him again. But…" Approaching me she sniffed at the air surrounding my being. "I smell two other humans as well. Did you feed?"
"No. I visited Emrik's parents."
Her eyebrows raised, "Did you kill his father?"
"I wish but sadly, no."
"What did you do?"
Seating myself before my vanity I began to run a brush through my tangled hair. "When I visited their house I found him beating Emrik's mother. When I entered into the home the man made the mistake of trying to hit me." I shook my head. "Anyways, I did not harm him, though I should have. I simply told him to leave and never return."
"Sounds too easy." Desdemona said with disbelief.
"Once I showed him what I truly was, it proved easy to persuade him."
"Ah, I see." Nodding her head she returned to her bed.
"What did you do while I was gone?"
"Locked myself away in here. I felt as though I would die of boredom." She let out a groan.
"You could have roamed about the castle if you wished or went out to feed. You do not have to stay locked away within this room." Once I had finished brushing my hair I stripped off my clothing and climbed into bed.

A Questionable Queen
Chapter Eight

"And what are your plans for the evening, Nehemiah?" The queen had stopped us in the hallway. Her dark brow was raised in question.

"Desdemona and I are going to feed."

The queen's eyes shifted over to Desdemona. "You've been leaving the castle every evening recently. You should not be that thirsty."

"I'm not. It's nice to break free of the castle and roam in the night." I said.

Her eyes questioned me. "I suppose I can understand that. Be careful, my daughter." With that, she returned to her chamber closing the door behind her.

Curiosity was eating away at my mind. Questions arose. My daughter could be a sneaky one. Still, I wondered about Desdemona. Something was odd about her. She was said to be a fledgling but I sensed something more. Something much older about that woman. Something that reminded me much of a woman whom I hated long ago. My nails tapped along the dark stone wall as I thought more about the strange acting of my daughter. Ever since Desdemona was brought here, Nehemiah has been different. More *careful,* I should say. More secretive. Though I was able to read emotions well, it was hard to read Nehemiah's. She was well guarded. Careful to keep her emotions within. Though she was my most adored child, she still had to be reminded of the punishments I could give.

Calling for a servant, a young girl rushed into my chamber. "Send out a man to keep watch on Nehemiah. Tell him to report back to me once he spies anything interesting."

Bowing she said, "Yes, your majesty."

I had hoped for Nehemiah's sake, no punishments would have to be dealt out.

Once again, I met Emrik in the clearing. He was there, waiting for me. Searching for me through the darkness of the night. The human had grown attached me, I knew this would happen. He was curious, such as humans were. It did not surprise me that he knew of vampires. My kind was spoken of in tales from long ago and carried on over the generations. Now the humans wrote books and filmed movies about us, though many depictions were far from right. I wondered, just what did he know of my kind?

Leaping down from the branch I had been perched on, I startled him. "Good evening." I said to him.

A smile crossed his lips, "Hey, Nehemiah." His emerald eyes peered over my shoulder. His brow creased in question, "Who's that?"

Desdemona approached us and stood by my side. "You've seen

me before, have you already forgotten?"

"No, but I don't know who you are." Emrik said.

"She is my daughter, Desdemona."

Emrik's eyes widened with surprise. "I-I didn't know you had kids. I didn't know vampires could *have* kids."

A chuckle escaped me. "Yes we have children but it is not the same as human's giving birth."

"Then how?"

"Tell me, what do you know about my kind?"

"Only what I've seen in movies." He admitted.

"And what have you seen in movies?"

A laugh escaped him, "You afraid of garlic?"

A scoff sounded from my lips as my eyes rolled. "Do you honestly believe that to be true?"

"Well, now I don't. What about sunlight?"

"That proves true. It is deadly to us."

Desdemona grasped my arm tightly. Her nails dug into my skin. She whispered into my ear, "Why are you telling him of us?"

My eyes met with hers in warning. I spoke in a low voice. "He already knows what I am. And what I tell him is none of your concern."

"If the queen were to find out, it would be her concern."

My brow raised to her, "Do you plan on telling her?"

She released her hold on me, "No."

Before I could continue on with my conversation with Emrik, the sound of a twig snapping caught my attention. Glancing over at Desdemona, I knew she had not heard it. Her ears were not as well trained as mine. I would have dismissed this sound as an animal prowling around but deep inside of my being, I knew it was no animal. It was a creature of my kind. A man. He was searching for me. He was getting close, too close. There was no time to run. I had to make it appear like I was feeding from Emrik, make it appear as though we were not speaking.

My voice sounded with panic. "Emrik, I'm going to drink your blood. I don't have time to explain. Trust me."

He didn't have time to respond. My teeth were already sinking into his flesh. Piercing through his neck. Warm blood cascaded down my throat. It swept across my tongue, igniting my taste buds. The sweet nectar of life caused my mind to explode in ecstasy. My body began to thrum with pleasure. The beast inside of me howled. A moan sounded from Emrik. That sound ignited my soul, my being. I felt the pleasure inside of me unlocking. Like the vault door was slowly opening allowing my want for affection to come flooding out. My body craved his. I wanted to feel his skin against mine. Only Emrik's blood had this effect upon my being. No other blood aroused me such ways.

Pushing away the pleasure, I focused my senses around me. The vampire man was nearby. Perched high up in a tree. I could hear his steady breathing, I could feel his questioning gaze weighing down upon me. He was curious, confused. It rippled off his being and through the air. Still, I continued to drink Emrik's blood. But I did so, slowly. Once the vampire man had left, I retracted my fangs and stepped away from Emrik. His neck was bleeding, there were puncture marks upon his skin. I had hurt him. His hand reached up and touched his injured neck. He winced when his fingers came into contact with it.

"What happened?" He questioned.

"Someone was spying on me. I had to do that so they wouldn't know we were speaking." I answered.

"Why would someone spy on you?"

"For reasons I cannot explain to you. Emrik, you know too much already." Saying this, I grabbed Desdemona by the hand and disappeared into the night. The sound of Emrik's voice calling out my name chased after us into the forest.

"My queen." The man had returned.

"What did you see?"

"It appeared as though she were meeting with a human but then she began to feed from him. She possibly lured him out to the woods to feed, nothing interesting." He spoke.

A sigh escaped my lips. My fingers trailed across the silky blanket creating spiral patterns. "From now on, whenever she leaves the castle you are to follow her. Understood?"

"Understood, my queen." He bowed his head, causing his brunet hair to fall into his crystal blue eyes. He was a handsome man.

"I suppose I could reward you for doing this job for me." My voice whispered seductively from my lips as I stood from my bed and approached the man.

His eyes took me in. His desire for pleasure was aroused. All men's true weakness. The way into their heart and mind. The way to wrap them around your finger like puppet strings. My fingers slid across the velvet fabric of my robe and pulled on the belt that tied it around my waist. Slowly the robe fell down onto the dark flooring, pooling around my feet. Stepping closer to him, my fingers gripped his chin. His eyes met with mine. My lips placed a tender kiss upon his lips.

Then I whispered into his ear, "Take your pick of one of the servants."

I could feel the disappointment radiating from his being. He thought he was to have me in bed. Ha, what a fool. Bowing his head, he left my chamber. I approached my bed and stretched my body out upon the plush blanket. Then, slowly drifted off to sleep.

Leaping into the treetop, I seated myself upon a branch. My head rested in the palms of my hands. Emrik's blood still tasted within my mouth. The sweetness of it remained on my taste buds. But for now, that matter was not important. The matter of the spy was. Who was he? And who sent him to watch me? To follow me? Once I returned to the castle I would be able to figure out who it was. I remembered the man's scent. Would I confront him? I did not know just yet. In this situation, I would need to be careful. Now that I was being watched, I could no longer see the human man. It would put us both in danger. I should have stopped seeing him before but I could not help myself.

"What happened, Nehemiah?" Desdemona seated herself beside me.

"We were followed." I said without lifting my head from my hands.

"By who?"

"I don't know yet."

"Do you know why we were being followed?"

"I don't know that either." A frustrated sigh escaped my lips.

Gazing upon me she asked, "What do we do now?"

"Now, we return to the castle."

Standing on the branch, we leapt down to the ground. Our feet sank in the deep snow. We should have left sooner. The horizon was turning orange as the sun was rising. Faster we ran through the forest. Higher the sun rose. As we were crossing the bridge a beam of sunlight shone on my arm. My skin burned like it had been set on fire. A scream bellowed from me. My being was encased with pain. The skin upon my arm began to melt away. Desdemona's aura radiated with concern, fear. Acting quickly, she swung me over her shoulder and carried me inside the castle. As the doors were closing behind us the sun bathed the land in its holy light.

Carefully she placed my body down upon the cold, dark floor. A servant rushed to the queen's room once she caught sight of me. Still my arm felt as though it were encased in a fiery inferno. I knew it appeared gruesome, this was not the first time this has happened to me. The sun's light was truly lethal to vampires. The one advantage the vampire hunters had over us. Peering down at my arm I saw that the skin was melted away. Other parts of it were charred. The bone of my arm was visible. My blood had been cooked away. Looking into Desdemona's face I read her emotions. She feared for my well-being. My daughter cared about me. Though, it should not have taken me this long to see that. My other hand rested upon hers, I smiled to reassure her that all would be well.

Soon, the queen made her appearance. She hurried down the stairs and knelt by my side. Her eyes grew worried as they peered upon my injured arm, or what remained of it. Calling for Selene, she instructed her to fetch a body from the feeding room and bring it forth immediately. I watched as her bouncy, blonde ringlets disappeared from sight. Selene returned carrying a body slung over her shoulder. A chuckle escaped me. It was indeed an odd sight to see. A short young girl carrying a grown man's body over her shoulder. The queen moved aside and Selene placed the body beside mine. Returning to my side, the queen grasped one of the arms and stretched it toward me. The man's wrist was held before my mouth. "Drink, my daughter." The queen instructed me to feed. She too worried for my well-being.

Lifting my head from the ground, I placed my mouth upon the wrist. My fangs slowly sank into the warm flesh. Once they pierced through the skin, blood cascaded into my mouth. My mind soared with bliss as I drank my fill. My arm began to tingle. Breaking away from the wrist, I watched as new skin formed over my exposed bone. It laced together. Soon my injury was gone. Nothing remained of it. Not even a scar. Selene gathered the man's body and returned it to the feeding room. The queen helped me to stand.

"Nehemiah, you should have returned sooner." She spoke.

"I know, mother." Hardly did I call her mother. Only when things such as this happened.

A sigh escaped her as she shook her head. "Be more careful, my daughter." With those parting words, she returned to her chamber.

Desdemona and I were seated upon her bed. It still troubled her, witnessing what the sun had done to me. Witnessing me cry out with pain, seeing me be weak. Had she never experienced the pain the sun's light brought? Her eyes lingered upon my healed arm.

"You could have let me die."

Her eyes snapped up to meet with mine, "I couldn't let that happen."

"And why not? I turned you into a vampire, something you did not wish for. Revenge you could have had if you allowed me to perish in the sun's light."

"Did you wish to die?" She raised a fiery eyebrow to me.

A sigh escaped me, "Did I wish for it? No. Have I before? Yes."

"May I ask you something?" Desdemona questioned hesitantly.

"You may."

"What does death mean to you? To everyone, it means something different. I am curious as to what it means to you."

I broke my gaze away from hers and stared down into the palms of my hands. "Let me answer your question, with a question. When we die are we truly dead?"

Her brows creased together in confusion. "I don't understand."

A chuckled escaped me as I shook my head, "No, of course you don't. You're too young to understand such a question."

"Then make me understand."

Matching her gaze with mine I said, "When we die, are we truly gone from this world? Or, are we immediately born again into a new life? Is life truly over for us when our vessels that contain our souls are broken?"

"You believe in reincarnation?" she asked.

"I believe in many things."

"Do you believe Emrik is a reincarnation of your lost lover?"

A sigh escaped me, "I strongly wish it to be true."

"Since you are being followed now, what are you going to do about the human?" Many questions she had.

"I have to stop meeting him. His life will be put into danger, I don't want to risk it again. Even if he might be my lover's reincarnation. I will not drag him back into the life of vampires."

A Past Lover

Chapter Nine

The next evening, I had planned to meet with Emrik. To say my final goodbye to him. Desdemona would disguise herself as I, wearing a cloak she would exit the castle through the doors. The man would follow after her, thinking Desdemona to be me. That would give me time to see Emrik and make it back to the castle before anyone suspected anything. Hopefully, this plan would prove successful.

Once Desdemona left the castle, I leapt down from my high balcony and dashed into the woods. Traveling swiftly through the night, I was careful to keep my distance from Desdemona's false trail. This was reckless, rebellious. But I enjoyed the thrill of it. Pushing the limits of the queen's word, though I knew I should not. I must tread carefully if I wish to keep my heart within my chest.

There, standing in the center of the clearing, was Emrik. My heart ached as I gazed upon him. Tonight, I would say goodbye. No longer would I see him. Maybe in the next life, we would meet once again. Or maybe not. No one knew what came after death once our lives were over. Though, I strongly believed that souls never truly vanished. They were simply placed inside new bodies, new vessels to call home. Perhaps my lover's soul was inside Emrik's body. Being given a new life, maybe he lost memories of his past. I strongly wished for it to be true, that Emrik was my lost lover that has come back to me. After all these years we had found each other again. Our souls searching far and wide. And yet, fate was working its cruel hands against us once more.

As I approached him, his face lit up with happiness. Making this all harder to say goodbye. He stepped toward me, he spread his arms out wide in an attempt to hug me. Emrik has not tried this before in the other times we had met one another. Though I strongly wished to step into his warm embrace, to feel his arms around me, I could not do it. Sensing something was wrong, his face creased with concern.

"Nehemiah, is something wrong?" His sweet voice spoke my name. The same voice my former lover had.

"Do you believe that lovers souls find one another again even after death?"

He was thrown off by my odd question but he answered it anyway. "I believe that."

My heart ached. "I do as well."

His warm hands grasped my shoulders carefully. I peered into those emerald eyes of his, I grew lost in his gaze. "What's wrong?" He asked.

Shaking my head I said, "This is goodbye, Emrik."

"Why are you saying goodbye?"

My hand reached up and caressed his cheek. A saddened smile formed on my lips. "Because fate has decided."

"Nehemiah, I don't understand." His eyes pleaded to me.

My lips placed a tender, sweet kiss upon his moist lips. Love and heart-ache blossomed inside of my chest. All at once my frozen heart warmed and the ice encasing it melted away. But then again, the ice would form over it once more. Perhaps it was karma paying me back for all the bad I have done in my life. Perhaps I deserved this kind of torture. Once again, my lover was being taken away from me. Life was playing a painful game and it was winning.

Pulling my lips away from his, Emrik's eyes stared upon me. Taking in every detail of my face. His fingers reached toward my hair and gently brushed through my dark locks. "I don't want to say goodbye." His voice whispered to me. His warm hand cupped around my cheek, his thumb gently tracing along my cold skin.

"We must." My words whispered from my lips. I pressed my cheek into the palm of his hand, breathing in his scent. Feeling his warmth against my skin.

"Why?"

"Your life is in danger, Emrik, because of me. Because of what I am."

"I'm not afraid of you." Though, he should be.

Shaking my head slightly, I said. "I know. But it is not me that will harm you, but others of my kind."

Then he spoke the words I feared he would say. Asking something from me that I refused to give him. "Then turn me into a vampire."

I backed away from him, his hand dropping from my face. "No. I will not do this to you."

"But it's what I want." He approached me once more.

Suddenly, the sound of Desdemona's voice rang out through the silent night. It was desperate, pleading, terrified. Her voice screamed my name, *"Nehemiah!"*

It was a warning, but of what? I would find out all too soon. A blur of motion emerged from the darkness of the forest. It was aimed at Emrik. He was unaware. Acting quickly, I rushed to save him, but I was a second too late. In the blink of an eye, Emrik's body was sent flying through the air. His body slammed into a nearby tree. I could hear the bones in his back fracturing, shattering like glass. It rang in my ears, the grinding of the bone, the snapping sound it made. He slumped down to the snowy ground, he was barely holding onto life. His breathing was labored. One of his lungs was punctured by a broken rib. Blood was filling it.

My heart ached to run to him, to save him from the pain he felt. But I could not do such. The matter of the vampire man was still at hand. Facing the man, anger blazed through my being, burning through my veins. Fire ignited within my eyes. This vampire would perish for what he has done. A smirk formed across his lips, he was proud of what he had done. He grew cocky, his ego was large. A laugh escaped him.

"I never would have guess that the *princess* had a love for filth such as humans. Hasn't anyone ever told you not to play with your food?"

I lunged at him. My fangs revealed, my nails long and sharp. He stood no chance against me. I was more powerful, stronger. In an instant, I was on top of him. His body crashed to the ground. A moan of pain escaped him as my nails dug into his shoulders. Blood oozed from the wounds and painted my fingers in crimson. The beast inside of me was awakened. It howled with the urge to kill. And kill, I would. My hand gripped around the man's throat. Slowly, my grasp tightened. His air supply was being cut off. He choked and gasped for air. But he would not die this way. Another, more pleasing way, crossed my mind. A malicious smile crossed my lips. My other hand removed itself from his shoulder, my nails dripping with his blood. Raising it into the air, I saw that fear grew in the man's blue gaze. His lips formed the words of; *no* and *mercy*. A bitter laugh escaped me, I sounded crazed. And maybe I was. He was a fool to think I would show him mercy. Piercing through his chest, my hand found its way around his heart. It beat crazily between my fingers. Locking my gaze with his, I slowly removed his heart. Blood spurted into the air and drizzled like crimson rain. His chest was an empty cavity. His blue eyes glossed over. He was dead. His soul had left its vessel. I had hoped that it would get lost along the currents of the wind, never again to call another body home.

I tossed his heart upon the ground next to his corpse. It splattered across the snow. Speckles of crimson dotted the white ground. Standing from the body, I hurriedly rushed over to Emrik's side. He was still alive but he was in so much pain. Agony creased his handsome face. Gently, I pulled his body into my lap. My hand rested upon his cheek as I stared into those emerald eyes of his. A hint of a smile crossed his lips as he gazed into my face.

Tears swelled in my eyes, "Why do you smile at a time like this?"

Every word he spoke caused him pain. "Because Nehemiah, you'll be the last thing I see before I die."

I shook my head. My tears landed on his cheeks. "No, don't speak like that. You shall live. Don't leave me again." Now, I was speaking to my past lover, Nathaniel. Pleading to him not to leave me again.

"Turn me into a vampire, please." He pleaded.

I shook my head. "I cannot force this kind of life upon you. I don't want you to be turned into a monster like I."

"Nehemiah, you aren't a monster." His eyes were sincere.

Desdemona approached from the darkness of the forest. Her eyes grew wide as she peered upon the human within my arms. She rushed to my side. "Is he going to live?" She asked.

Meeting her gaze, my eyes told her the answer to her question. But she shook her head, there was a way. Emrik could survive this. But it was not the life I wanted him to live. "Nehemiah…" His painful voice whispered my name.

My eyes met with his, "Yes?" My voice shook.

"Turn me."

My gaze turned away from his as I met with Desdemona's. "Tell me how to do it." She said.

Moving Emrik from my lap, I gently lay him upon the ground. Desdemona moved beside him and lifted his head. "When you bite him, bite down on your tongue and transfer your blood into his veins."

Desdemona leaned down to Emrik's neck. Her fangs revealed themselves and pierced through his skin. His face creased with more pain. Blood trickled down his neck from the bite wound. Desdemona was quick to end this and relieve Emrik of his pain. She pulled away from his neck and moved from his side, allowing me to be beside him. Gently, I grasped his hand in mine own. When turning into a vampire, you die. But then you are reborn. I brought his hand up to my face. I wanted to reassure him. To let him know all would be well. Emrik's eyes met with mine before he closed them. His life as human has ended. Soon his life as a vampire would begin.

As his human life came to a close and Desdemona's blood pumped through his veins, his body began to heal itself. The bones formed together once more. The bruises that blossomed upon his skin faded away. His eyes fluttered open. Their emerald color vanished and was replaced with crimson. My heart was saddened. I would miss staring into those bright green eyes. As I stared into his eyes something felt older about them. A sense of familiarity washed over me. My soul seemed to reach out for his. Could it be?

"My love…" He whispered to me.

"Nathaniel?" My mind was like a whirlwind. How was it possible? Did my love really return to me?

A smile spread across his lips. "I have found you once more. My soul has been searching for yours."

My heart lit aflame with love. It pounded joyously within my chest. "I knew you would return for me." Tears burned within my eyes.

He stood from the ground and offered me his hand. Placing my hand in the palm of his, he lifted me from the ground. Our bodies were drawn together. His arms wrapped me in an embrace. My eyes locked with his. My mind was still in disbelief. But my soul knew it had found its other half. He was the missing piece of my puzzle. He completed me. As tears of happiness burned down my cheek, Nathaniel's gentle fingers wiped them away.

"Why do you cry, my love?" His voice reverberated throughout my being. My soul thrummed with the sound of it.

"For so long, I believed that you were dead and gone from this world. For so long, I wished for you to return to me. Now here you stand before my eyes, alive and mine once again."

"In every life, I shall always find you." His hands grasped a gentle hold on either side of my face. His thumbs tracing along my skin. He brought his face down to mine. My heart pounded crazily as his lips came closer. After hundreds of years, I would once again kiss the lips of my lover.

As our lips met, the scent of love swirled around within the air surrounding us. Roses with a hint of honey. The smell I would never forget. Our very essences seemed to meld together. Our souls reaching out and grasping one another. It seemed as though, no matter how close our bodies were, we wanted to be closer to one another. As if our souls wanted to leave the vessels we called home. Leave these bodies and drift together along the currents of the wind. I wished we could do such. But I would begin to miss the feel of his skin against mine. I would miss kissing his ever sweet lips.

Two Lives, One Soul
Chapter Ten

"What became of Emrik's soul?" I questioned Nathaniel.

"Emrik's soul is my soul. We are one in the same."

"So, Nehemiah, Emrik was a reincarnation of your past lover." Desdemona said. She was seated high up upon a branch, her legs dangled within the air.

"What was it like, the other world?" I was hesitant to ask that question for I feared the answer. Was it a wonderful place or were vampires truly damned to the underworld?

His brows creased together as he thought deeply. "I do not remember. Once I crossed back into this world, my memories of death vanished."

A sigh escaped my lips, "It seems as though the living aren't meant to know of the world of the dead."

Nathaniel's hand came to rest upon mine. My eyes gazed upon our hands. I had missed this man so much. Throughout the years my soul yearned for only him. "Do not worry yourself with thoughts of the other world." His words spoke to me.

"How long did your soul travel until it found a new body?"

His now crimson eyes turned to look upon the vast galaxy above us. "Many, many years. My soul drifted along the wind, traveling across lands and oceans. Finally, my soul was dragged down from the sky and attached itself to a baby's body. That was the day, Emrik was born." Once more his eyes gazed upon me. "I was reborn."

"Tell me, why didn't your soul awaken before you were turned?"

A smirk crossed his lips as his hand rested upon my cheek. "Because I was destined to be a vampire. Much like you, my love." Nathaniel turned serious once more. "As Emrik, I always knew you were out here somewhere within this world. Before I found you as a human, I had dreamt of you nearly every night." Sadness and guilt flickered within his eyes. "I am truly sorry. I had made love to another woman. Within my heart I hold a deep regret."

My hand caressed his cheek. "My love, do not apologize. You did not know. I did not know you would return. We have both made our mistakes."

His lips placed a kiss in the palm of my hand. "I vow to be ever faithful to you, until the end of my days."

"I vow as well."

Leaping down from the tree branch she was perched on, Desdemona approached. "I hate to break up this lovely reunion but the sun will rise soon."

"And now we return to the castle." I stood from the log we had been sitting on.

Desdemona raised a fiery brow to me. "And what do we tell the queen?" She gestured to Nathaniel and the dead vampire.

"We tell her he is my child." I turned my back to her and began to walk away. "As for the vampire, we act as though we don't know anything."

"You think she will believe that? First you turn me, now you say you turned him. She will grow suspicious, Nehemiah."

"There is nothing else I could say."

She approached me, "Tell her I turned him."

A deep sigh escaped me. "When one of her children creates another child of their own, they are only allowed to turn one person. She believes you have only just been turned and then you suddenly decide to change someone? She won't believe that."

"Why has she put these restrictions upon us?"

"She is the queen and her word is law. That is all we know."

Nathaniel approached me. "You still live with the queen?"

Long, long ago Nathaniel and I dreamed of leaving the castle and traveling the world together. But that dream was destroyed when Nathaniel was murdered before my eyes. "I do."

"Did you ever travel the world?"

"I did not."

Grasping ahold of his hand, I led the way through the forest. I wouldn't risk being caught in the sun's light again. As the castle appeared in sight, nervousness began to eat away at my mind. Would the queen finally see through my lies? And if so, what would she do to me? To Desdemona and Nathaniel? Fear clawed at my being, raking its long nails across my soul. A sickened feeling swelled within my gut. Nathaniel tightened his grip on my hand. He was the only person who could feel my emotions, the only one attuned to them. He knew I was nervous. He knew I feared for our lives. Nathaniel has witnessed the queen's cruelty many times before. He feared her, as did many vampires.

Once we entered into the castle, I let go of Nathaniel's hand. We had to act as though we were not lovers in order for this to work. Curious eyes glanced our way as we ascended the staircase and approached the queen's chamber. Desdemona and Nathaniel quickly calmed their emotions. Coolness rippled through the air around them, it was almost as though a slight breeze radiated from their beings. My knuckles lightly knocked upon the queen's door, opening it we entered inside her chamber. There she stood in front of her mirror. A thin black robe covered her body. Her blue eyes gazed upon us from the mirror's reflection. Her dark brow raised in question. Turning to face our small group, she glided across the floor and stood before me. Her eyes shifted over to Nathaniel, still his emotions were calm.

"Another fledgling I see." She waltzed around Nathaniel. "And is this one your child as well?" She leaned closer to him and sniffed at the air around him.

"Yes."

"Interesting. And I presume you wish for him to stay in your chamber as well?" She questioned me.

I nodded my head to her.

"Soon it shall become crowded in there if you continue making children." She approached me once more. The queen gazed down upon me, her voice grew stern. "Remember my daughter, five is the limit."

"I remember."

"Good. I'll have a servant prepare a bed for him." With that, she dismissed us from the room.

Selene prepared another bed. It was placed beside Desdemona's. Nathaniel would not need the bed, of course. Together we would slumber upon mine. The same bed that Nathaniel and I had made love on many times before in the past. He remembered it well, a chuckle escaped him as he eyed the bed. Approaching one of the bed posts, a smile spread across his lips.

"I see you still have not repaired this bedpost." He peered over his shoulder at me with a mischievous look upon his face.

"Why would I? That broken post represents a very *pleasing* memory." Approaching him from behind, I wrapped my arms around him. I stood on my tip-toes and whispered loving in his ear, "That night was filled with love."

"I remember." His lips whispered.

Desdemona cleared her throat loudly, causing us to turn our attention upon her. "Do I need to sleep in another room tonight?"

Giggles of laughter sounded from Nathaniel and I. "No my daughter. Tonight will not be filled with love making." Glancing at my lover I add, "Though I wish it was."

"Thank God." Desdemona said as her body fell onto the mattress of her bed.

"Do not thank a god that hates our kind." I said sharply. Hatred burned brightly throughout my being when *God* was spoken of.

Propping her head upon her hand she gazed upon me with her ghostly eyes, "You know hunters learn the word of God. Worship him. They believed that he put them here on this earth to destroy our kind."

Seating myself before my vanity, I began to braid my hair. "Perhaps he did. Perhaps we truly are the devil's children." My voice sounded with coldness.

Nathaniel approached in the mirror's reflection, his hand rested upon my shoulder. "They say God forgives all." His voice spoke softly to me.

A sigh escaped my lips. "Then I can only hope that our souls aren't truly damned."

Nathaniel leaned down and placed a tender kiss upon the crown of my head. "Come, let us rest my love."

Nathaniel had swept me off my feet and carried my body within his strong arms. Gently, he laid me down upon the bed. His crimson eyes stared endearingly upon me. I grew lost within his gaze. His lips came closer to mine and they planted a sweet, sweet kiss upon my lips. Once more, love blossomed within my chest like flowers blooming in the spring time. A wave of heat rushed over my being. But nothing more came from the kiss. Tonight we shall not make love. We would enjoy one another's presence. Breath in each other's scent.

Nathaniel wrapped his arms around my small body as I placed my head upon his chest. Slowly my eyes closed, my vision encased with darkness. Within my ears sounded the beating of my lover's heart. Its steady drumming was evidence enough that he was truly alive. He had truly come back to this world from the other, searching for me. Drifting along the wind lost in time. Wondering the world searching for his soul's other half. He had found me. Now, forever could be ours like we had promised each other many years ago.

A Prisoner in My Own Home
Chapter Eleven

The sound of Desdemona and Nathaniel's startled screaming awoke me from my ever sweet dreams. When my eyes had opened, I gazed around the room. Four vampire men had forced open my door and stormed into the chamber. Two men held Desdemona down upon the floor, holding her arms behind her back. One of the men pressing her face down to the ground with the bottom of his boot. The remaining two men came after Nathaniel. Acting quickly, I lunged from my side of the bed throwing myself at the vampires. My body slammed into one of the men causing us to go toppling down to the cold, hard ground. Before I could sink my sharp nails into the man's neck, a pair of strong arms wrapped around my body and pulled me off the man. Soon I found myself air born. I hurtled across the room and my body slammed into the hard stone wall, my skull cracked against it. Stars danced before my eyes as I slumped onto the floor. Nathaniel yelled my name. He attempted to come to my aid but the men had him down in matter of seconds.

As I tried to stand, the queen entered into the chamber. Her ghostly eyes glanced over at Desdemona and Nathaniel. She slightly shook her head as she broke her gaze away from them. Soon her eyes found me. Anger lit aflame within her gaze. She bounded across the room in a spilt second. Her boney fingers found themselves around my neck. My body was hefted from the floor and held against the wall. Her nails dug into my skin as they grew. Her face was hardened with anger. Then I knew, she had seen through my lies. Unmasked the truth. Now, she would deal out a punishment for each one of us. I feared not for myself but for the lives of Desdemona and Nathaniel.

"No more lies, Nehemiah. Tell me the truth about Desdemona." Her voice was stern with a coldness that escaped her lips like a breath of frost. A chill crept along my spine.

"You already know of the truth."

Her fingers tightened around my throat. I winced with pain as her nails pierced into my skin. "I wish to hear it from *your* lips."

My eyes glanced over at my daughter. Within her gaze held strength, no fear could be found within her ghostly eyes. But a flicker of hope burned within them. She had faith that I would protect her. After all, a mother protects her children. "She was a hunter, from my mother's bloodline." I spoke the truth.

Her face contorted with disgust. "How old is she?"

"One hundred and fifty five."

The queen drew her arm back with her hand still clutched around my throat, and slammed my head against the wall. My skull cracked but it wasn't an injury that would kill me. My vision was encased with darkness. Consciousness drifted away from me for a second as I slumped onto the floor by the queen's feet. She paced uneasily throughout my chamber. She did not understand why I would betray our kind in such a way. Turning our mortal enemy into one of us. It went against everything we believed. We fought and killed hunters, never turning them. For if we did, it would bring a disgrace to our kind. And I have done this very disgrace. I had gone against the queen and my people.

The queen approached Nathaniel, the two men were still holding him down. She kneeled to the ground before him. Her fingers brushed away his dark locks that had fallen into his crimson eyes. "I thought I had gotten rid of you. But of course you had to be stubborn and return."

"You did not kill me. A hunter did." Nathaniel spoke.

A bitter chuckle escaped the queen's lips as she shook her head. "Ah, yes. A hunter did kill you but because I asked for him too." She winked a ghostly eye at him and stood from the ground.

The queen knew that Nathaniel had returned, but how? Now I learn that she is also the reason behind his death. Confusion swirled around my mind. Why would she order him killed? Why would she do such a thing to me? To her daughter? I couldn't understand. She was the reason behind my suffering. She caused me this pain and grief that I have been carrying around for hundreds of years. I had blamed myself for his death but I wasn't the one at fault. The queen was, my *mother* was.

"Why?" I asked.

She peered over her shoulder at me. "He was going to take you away from me. I would not allow that to happen."

"You killed him for your own selfish reasons!" As I shouted I noticed that tears had fallen from my eyes. Now I knew what betrayal felt like. I had been betrayed by the woman I have admired for so long. Betrayed by someone I called mother.

My shouted words did not faze her. "Your place is here, Nehemiah. You are the princess and you are also *my* daughter."

"You cannot keep me here forever! My life is my own!"

The queen approached me, knelt before me, and slapped me across the face. My cheek throbbed with stinging pain. "You will not shout at me any longer. Your life has never been your own. Your life is mine. I gave to you the gift of eternal life."

Spitting out a clump of blood, I peered into the queen's eyes with hatred written within my gaze. "You played a trick on my human mind. Using my unsatisfying life and dislike for my mother to your advantage. You weaved your way into my thoughts."

She leaned down to me and placed a kiss upon my brow. "A suitable punishment is in order. A hundred years locked away will teach you to never disobey your mother again."

As she approached the door she glanced back into the room. "As for Desdemona, there will be an execution in the court yard tomorrow evening."

"No! Don't punish her for my doing! I beg of you!" I pleaded loudly for the queen to revoke her punishment. Desdemona was my daughter, and I cared for her as much as I cared for Nathaniel. I wanted to protect her, to keep her safe.

Turning her face away from me, she said, "This is also your punishment. Some day you will learn, Nehemiah." As she left the room, two more men filed in behind her. They approached me and snatched my body from the cold floor. I was being dragged away from my lover, and my daughter. My little family. I would do anything to protect them but now, I was powerless. There was nothing I could do to save them from the queen's wrath.

Desdemona's eyes were the last one's I gazed into before I was dragged down the hallway. Still within her eyes burned that fiery flame of hope. She still believed that I would save her. A mother always saved their children. But I would fail. I was not fit to be a mother and it was my fault that Desdemona would be killed come tomorrow. My heart ached as I forced my gaze away from Desdemona's.

Shackles
Chapter Twelve

The room was dark, the smell of decay fumed within the small chamber. Heavy shackles were chained around my wrists and ankles. They rattled across the stone floor. My body was nude, stripped of my clothing. All around me were chained criminals. Though the room was dark, my eyes could still see their morphed faces. No longer were they the beautiful creatures spoken of in tales. Their timeless beauty had been stolen from them. They were nothing but boney, skeletal things. That was to be my fate as well.

All around the room were scattered bones from victims. Humans from our feedings. The criminals had gnawed the bones clean, stripping the flesh away from the bodies. Had consuming flesh driven these criminals mad? Would I soon be just as mad as they are? A hundred years was my punishment. Many of these vampires have been here for centuries, some never to leave this chamber again. Beside me sat the man who nearly brought our kind to extinction. He was the reason the human armies marched to our castle. He was the very reason for the many battles that took place here.

As my eyes gazed upon him, I was startled at how distorted and aged his face had become. Never have I entered into this room before. For the first time in years, I was gazing upon Raymond's face. His cheeks had caved in, so thin his face appeared. Wrinkles formed deep creases around his ghostly eyes. His once sandy hair now streaked with silver. His arms and legs were nothing but skin and bone. His ribs exposed. I felt pity for the man seeing him in this state. But it was a fitting punishment.

His breathing was labored as he spoke to me. "Princess Nehemiah, a surprise it is seeing you chained within this chamber." I noticed his teeth had blackened, some had already rotted away. His breath reeked foully.

"It is a surprise to see you are still alive."

A smirk formed across his thinned lips. "Most unfortunate, is it not?" A chuckle escaped him.

"I never understood why you betrayed your own kind." I said to him.

"Because, God said I would be forgiven. All of us would be forgiven." Raymond was once a man of God, a priest.

Gesturing around the room I said, "Where is your *God* now?"

Leaning his head against the wall a peaceful smile formed upon his lips. "Ah, he is here. Within this very chamber. He is everywhere but also nowhere."

"You aren't making much sense."

A maddened laugh escaped him. "Don't you see? He is the very essence of life."

"Life is the essence of life. A god created from the minds of humans is not."

"Ah, a nonbeliever I see. Have you ever met God?" He leaned in closer to me. A sickening feeling arose in my stomach. I had to suppress the urge to retch.

My brow raised in question to him. "Have you ever met him?"

He shrugged his shoulders. "You have me there, princess."

"How can you believe in something if you cannot see it?"

He turned his gaze to me, "That's what it means to believe. To have faith in something that you know within your soul exists even though you may not be able to see it now."

A bitter scoff escaped me. "Now? Meaning you think that God has forgiven you?"

"Ah, not yet he hasn't. Not until I have laid our souls to rest."

"So, we really are the devils children."

He tried to reach out for me with his hand, but the shackles stopped him from doing so. I did not need his reassurance or pity. "What is your sentence?" He asked.

"A hundred years."

"Is that all? I say you got off rather lucky."

"But my daughter is also being put to death for my crime."

"God will forgive her when her soul leaves this world."

I lashed out with anger, "Stop speaking of a God that cares not for our kind!"

Raymond withdrew his still reaching hand. "If it's not God that you believe in then tell me, what is?"

A sigh escaped me. "I used to believe in the queen."

"And now you do not?"

I shook my head.

"You have finally learned she is not the queen worth admiring."

"Learned too late."

"It is never too late, young princess."

A scoff escaped me, "Young? I'm nearly a thousand years old."

"Young at soul and heart." His eyes glanced down at the shackles around my wrists and ankles. "You have the strength to break free, why don't you?"

"The punishment would be worse if I tried to escape."

Then the door to the chamber room opened. Candle light flickered inside the room. Entering was the queen. Hisses rang out around me, echoing within the small room. The queen paid them no mind as she glided across the floor, careful to not trip on any bones.

Standing before me she addressed me, "Hello my daughter."

"What do you want?"

A sigh escaped her as she shook her head. "Maybe time in here will erase that attitude."

"Or make my hatred for you flourish." I smiled sarcastically to her.

When she said nothing more I asked, "Why are here?"

"I came here hoping to learn the rest of the truth."

"And what truth would that be?"

She crossed her arms over her pale, large breasts. "I know you did not turn Nathaniel."

"I did not."

"And that Desdemona did."

"It seems to me that you already know the truth. You have just wasted your time coming here."

"I also came here hoping to find *my* Nehemiah. Not your past mother's Alexandria." She raised a dark brow to me.

"I am no one's piece of property."

"Do you remember that night when you were turned?"

Glancing up to the queen I said, "How could I forget?"

A saddened sigh escaped her plump lips. "On that night, I had planned to kill you."

"Why did you plan too?"

Her eyes examined me closely. "I was going to murder you out of revenge but then I saw a lot of myself in you."

I grew confused, "Revenge for what?"

The queen paced along the stone ground before me. "Your

mother was a vampire hunter. She had murdered my dearest friend. So in turn, I planned on killing someone she held dear."

"You should have went through with your plan." I said bitterly.

Her eyes gazed deeply into mine, "Maybe I should have."

Stretching my arms out wide I said, "Then do it now. Carry out your plan of revenge. Strike me down."

She hesitated. The queen couldn't kill me. She had grown attached to me. Maybe some sickened part of her mind did hold love and care for me. Or maybe a mother just couldn't kill her children. Or at least in the queen's sense, couldn't kill her favorite child. Finally, she turned her back to me. Approaching the door, she called out over her shoulder, "In a hundred years I have hope that my old Nehemiah will be waiting for me." Then, the door silently closed behind her.

My mind was encased with an ever sweet dream. A dream of my lover, Nathaniel. It seemed so real, like he was actually near me. I could feel his breath upon my skin. I could hear his words whispering sweetly into my ears. But I knew that this was not my reality. My eyes fluttered open and stared into the darkness of the chamber. Labored breathing sounded all around me. My mind wondered when the next feeding would be. When would the bodies of the victims be tossed in here? The criminals would swarm around the corpses like flies, gnawing away at the flesh. I would not take part of that. Eating flesh disgusted me deeply. I would rather wither away than eat the meat of humans, something we once were at one point in time. Cannibalism was not something I was interested in trying.

The sounds from the feeding room were muffled. But my ears could hear well. The queen had taken the first bite of the feast. The group swarmed in on the victims and began to suck the blood from their veins. The beast inside of me howled with hunger. The craving for blood was immense. My throat burned for it. My mouth felt dry. The need for blood would cause me to cave in. I would be forced to consume the flesh from the corpses. Though the meat was no blood, it would keep me alive. I shook my head, I would not cave into those thoughts and cravings.

    Soon enough, the feast came to an end. The door was opened and in entered Selene. Her youthful face filled me with hope for some odd reason. Her blonde curls bounced as she waltzed into the room and dumped the hefty men onto the stone floor. They landed with muffled thuds. The criminal's chains were extended so that they may feast upon the corpses. As they devoured the flesh, I remained in my spot. My eyes watched as their rotted fangs tore into the skin. It was gruesome. Selene turned her head away from them and her round blue eyes found mine. Sympathy and pity washed over her gaze. Approaching me, she kneeled on the ground. Her hand reached out for mine and grasped it. Gently she gave me a reassuring squeeze. Leaning in close to me, she whispered into my ear, "I'll get you out of here." She winked a ghostly eye to me and hurriedly left the chamber and closed the door behind her.

    I wished I could believe her words. I wanted to believe that she could free me from this imprisonment. But, she wouldn't dare cross the queen. Selene shouldn't risk her life for mine.

Execution
Chapter Thirteen

The evening of Desdemona's execution had arrived. Two vampire men entered into the chamber and unhooked my shackles from the stone wall. However, they did not unchain my arms and ankles. The heavy shackles were still locked around my wrists. The chains scraped across the stone floor as they led me from the chamber. As I entered into the heart of the castle, many eyes gazed down upon me. Faint whispers filtered through the air and made their way into my ears. Many vampires agreed with my punishment while others felt as though the queen had gone too far. But of course, no one would dare speak against the queen's word. After all, it was law.

    The two men led me out of the castle and into the courtyard. Standing beside the massive marble fountain was the queen.

Desdemona was leaned over the side of the fountain, her hands tied behind her back. She could have fled, escaped this place but she still had hope I would save her. Her neck was exposed for the queen to deal out her execution. My daughter's ghostly eyes gazed upon me. A hint of a relieved smile formed across her lips. My heart ached. Deep within my heart I knew I could not save her. She would die here. Her immortal life would be ended all too soon. In a way, she was lucky. She would be freed from this castle and the queen. So, was this truly a punishment? Desdemona's soul would be freed. Allowed to travel across the wind and explore lands. Her essence would no longer be trapped inside its bodily vessel. It would be free, like all souls should be.

    Two other vampire men dragged out Nathaniel. The queen must have locked him inside my chamber to keep us separated. Relief washed over me like a cool wave to see him unharmed. Nathaniel's eyes saw me in chains and naked. Anger flared throughout the air around him. He was moved to stand beside me. I began to wonder why he was brought here. The queen dismissed the four men and soon it was only us four in the courtyard.

    She approached us, the sword she held within in her hand scraped across the ground behind her. Though she could kill Desdemona without the need of a sword, she preferred to use it. She loved to see and hear the sound of steel slicing through flesh and bone. Many times I have seen her execute her children with that very sword she held within her hand now. As she approached us I couldn't help but wonder where Selene was. She had promised to help me escape but now she was nowhere to be found. My only light of hope had flickered and died away.

    "Nehemiah, tonight your child is being executed. She is a hunter and you did our kind a disgrace by turning her into one of us. Do you have anything to say about yourself or your actions?" Her gaze was judgmental.

    Matching her gaze I said, "If you're asking if I am ashamed by my choice, then the answer is no. Desdemona is my daughter and I love her just like any *mother* should love their child."

Holding her chin up high she said, "And a mother takes responsibility for their children." She held the sword before me. The queen expected for me to strike down my own child. My eyes gazed down widely upon the steel weapon. A gut retching feeling swelled up inside of me. My mind pictured the sword within my grasp, pictured it slicing through Desdemona's neck. The sound of her head splashing into the water of the fountain sounded within my ears. I could see the water turning crimson as her blood contaminated the pure liquid.

I shook my head. "I will not murder her."

"You will do as you are commanded!" She shouted angrily at me.

Straightening my spine, I stared deeply into her eyes. "I no longer take commands from a woman that murders and throws her children in prison."

The queen's lips flattened into a thin line. "I see." She approached Nathaniel and my heart began to race. It felt as though it would burst through my chest. She raised the blade of the sword toward Nathaniel's throat and pressed it against his skin. "If you do not execute Desdemona, then I kill your lover. So what shall it be, *my daughter*?"

As my mind swarmed with a thousand thoughts, Desdemona spoke to me. "Nehemiah, kill me."

My eyes widened with shock at her request. "No. I cannot."

"I see fear within you. Fear in losing me and fear in losing Nathaniel. But I ask you, which one would hurt more? Losing me or your lover?"

My eyes glanced over at Nathaniel and back to Desdemona. "Both would hurt me greatly."

She shook her head, "That is not what I asked you."

A sigh escaped me. My heart knew the true answer. "Losing Nathaniel again would destroy me."

Desdemona understood my answer and feelings. "Then you know what to do."

Tears burned within my eyes. "Since when did you become wiser than me?"

A smile spread across her lips, "I learned from my mother."

The queen approached me once more. Without speaking a single word, she handed over the sword. It weighed heavily within my grasp. Not because I was weak but because of the burden I would carry with me for the remainder of my long life. Turning my back to the queen, I faced my daughter. She was ready to leave this life. Once more she smiled before facing her head down toward the water. Her neck was exposed. The sword would slice through it easily, like butter.

I was being forced to kill my one and only child. Tears burned down my cheeks as I raised the sword into the cold winter's air. My heart fell apart piece by broken piece. A choked sob escaped my lips as I spoke my final words to my daughter, "I love you, Desdemona."

"I love you as well, mother." Hearing her call me mother made this all harder. If only she had truly hated me, it would be so much easier.

Slowly, the sword sliced through the air. Inching closer to Desdemona's neck. But suddenly, something slammed into my side. Down I toppled to the ground. The sword clanged as it landed upon the stone ground. My back scraped across the stones, breaking skin. I knew my wounds wept with crimson. But my focus was not on that matter. Peering up, my eyes met with Selene's. A smile spread across her silky lips. "I told you I would help."

Beside us, a few feet away, the queen shouted out with anger. Servants stormed into the courtyard, along with some of the queen's children. They aimed their attacks at the queen. Though the group was massive, the queen could hold her own. Down fell many vampires at the queen's feet. The battle goddess she once was had been awakened. A dark shadow cast itself over her face as her eyes turned crimson and her fangs revealed themselves. She was a blur of terror. The group swarmed around their queen like angry wasps lashing out attacks.

Breaking free of his shackles, my lover rushed over to me. Selene hurriedly tore apart the rope that bound Desdemona's hands, though she could have done that herself. "We need to hurry." Selene glanced over at the failing vampires. "They won't hold up much longer."

"How did you convince them to go against the queen?" I asked with disbelief.

"Many people do not agree with the queen's law. So it was easy to get them to turn against her." Selene seemed rather proud of herself for convincing these vampires to turn against the woman that they called their queen.

But our hope of escape was destroyed when the queen swiftly beheaded all of the vampires who attacked her. Their heads landed before our feet, their ghostly eyes staring into ours. Death was looking upon us. Crimson pooled on the stone ground and soaked my bare feet in blood. Blinded rage filled the queen's face. Blood dripped from the tips of her crimson coated fingers. Her nails were long and sharp. In a blur, she crossed the space separating us within a matter of seconds. Her hand found itself around my neck. My hands gripped around her wrist trying to break free of her grasp. But she was so much stronger than I. Keeping her hold on me, she leapt into the dark night sky. Our gazes locked before we plummeted back down to the ground. She slammed my body into the stone. Stars twinkled before my blackened vision as my skull cracked against the hard, unforgiving ground. Blood formed within my mouth. Coughing, I spat it up upon the stone. It splattered across the ground. Still, the queen had a hold on me.

Within her crimson eyes held betrayal. Her first born had gone against her. She racked her brain trying to figure out why. "You are my daughter! How dare you do this to me! Your mother!" As she cried out angrily her grasp on my neck shook. She was fighting the urge to kill me. She was fighting herself. The queen was truly lost in thought, should she kill me? Or, allow me to live?

My voice hardened as I spoke. "I am not your daughter. You are no mother. You are the devil himself in disguise."

Anger flared throughout her being. Her aura rippling through the air around us. A flash of heat radiated from her body. Her crimson eyes seemed to glow. Never have I seen her this angry, this heartbroken over betrayal. "You shall learn to be obedient to the one who created you!"

My bloodied words spat from my lips, "You did not create me!" My knee slammed into the queen's stomach. She staggered backward, releasing her hold on me. On my feet I stood, ready to fight. She straightened herself. Her face turning stone cold. No longer did emotions blaze through her eyes, they were empty. Her aura was calm, deadly calm.

Desdemona, Nathaniel, and Selene moved to stand beside me. They were ready for a battle. But I could not put their lives on the line. "You all must flee."

"I will not leave you here to fight her alone, Nehemiah." Nathaniel's face was serious. I knew he would not leave but he must.

"You have to leave. I am the only one who stands a chance against the queen." I pleaded for him to go.

"No one is leaving here alive!" The queen shouted as she sprang forth.

Shoving Nathaniel away from her coming attack, I was hit full force. Her body slammed into mine. Together we were sent flying across the courtyard. Our limbs tangled together. My fangs revealed themselves. Sinking them into her flesh, she cried out with agony. Screeching in my eardrums. Soon we crashed into a stone wall, the rocks exploded all around us as we flew through it. As we rolled across the ground I was finally freed from the queen's grasp. Standing, I found that the beast inside of me had awakened. It was prepared for battle. Howling for blood. Howling for the thrill. My nails grew long and sharp. The queen was mine for the taking. No longer would she harm the people that I held dear to my heart. Her reign of cruelty would be brought to an end.

"So, is this how it's going to be, Nehemiah?" She asked as she stood from the ground.

"This is the only way it has to be, Persephone." It had been a great while since I had addressed the queen by her name. This symbolizing that I no longer claimed her as my mother or my queen.

Crouching down she said, "Then so be it."

We lunged at one another. Neither of us would hold back. This would be a fight to the death. Creator versus the created. Our bodies collided. My nails sank into the queen's side. Warmness coated my hand as her blood wept from the wound I had inflicted upon her. She hissed loudly. Her fingers wrapped around my wrist and tore my hand from her side. Deep wounds punctured her skin. Crimson leaked from them and stained her pale skin. Those injuries did not bother her for long, instantly the skin began to lace itself together once more. The bleeding had ceased. Not a scar was left behind, like I never had harmed her. This fight would prove to be difficult. My chances of winning were slim. Though, I was her first and strongest child, I was not as strong as the queen.

One thing I must keep well-guarded, was my heart. Leaving an opening to my chest, she would seize the chance to plunge her fist into my heart. My life would be ended all too easily. I mustn't allow her that chance. My arms moved to guard my chest, ready to block the queen's attacks. Her crimson eyes gazed up me, a smirk wrote itself upon her all too perfect lips. She shook her head as a chuckle escaped her. "I won't deny that you are my strongest child. But you must never forget that I am stronger."

"Oh, I haven't forgotten. But that doesn't mean I won't fight with every fiber of my being."

She shook her head once more, "The foolish never learn."

Striking out with her left leg, I raised an arm to block her attack. Wrapping my fingers around her ankle, I twisted her leg causing her to fall to the ground. She didn't remain down for long. She leapt into the sky and I followed after her. We circled each other within the cold air. The queen was careful, deciding which move she should make next. Which move would render me lifeless. Once more she struck out with her leg, only this time I was slow to counter the attack. Her foot made contact with my side and I was sent hurtling through the air. My body slammed into the side of the castle. Crimson obscured my vision. Cracks raced through the hard stone beneath my back. The breath was knocked from my lungs. I winced with pain but I couldn't remain down for long. The queen was flying toward me, her hand reaching for my open chest. Her nails ready to pierce through my skin. Springing forth from the wall, I aimed myself at her. My arms wrapped around her thin waist and we were both sent falling from the sky. Once more, we crashed into the ground. Only this time, I was the one on top. The queen was pinned beneath my body. Her face was morphed. Hatred, anger, betrayal, all those emotions were blazing through her at once. Creases formed around her deep crimson eyes. Dark circles blossomed beneath them. Hatred truly was an ugly thing. Distorting the faces of even the most beautiful of creatures. Angrily she hissed at me. Her nails raking against my skin trying to break free of my grasp. My side wept with crimson as her nails tore into my flesh. So much pain I was in. But I couldn't give up.

    My fist made contact with her cheek. My knuckles cracked against her skin. The bone of her skull cracked. Blood splattered across the stone from her mouth. She turned to face me once more. Her bone repaired itself, her cheek no longer caved into her face. A crazed smile spread across her bloodied lips. Crimson coated her pearly teeth.

    "You cannot kill me! Ha, I knew you were weak!" She lifted her head from the ground and brought her face closer to mine, "Weak just like your pathetic, deranged mother." Spit and blood sprayed across my face as the queen spat at me.

    Her hand moved quickly, breaking the bone in my forearm. A yelp of pain escaped me. The sound of my bone cracking echoed within my ears. I toppled over in agony. The queen seized her chance and was on top of me in an instant. It was true, I was weak. I couldn't bring myself to end the life of my creator. My weakness, my hesitation, would prove to be fatal. My life was within the queen's grasp now. A wicked grin crossed her lips as her hand made its way down to my chest. As the bone in my arm slowly began to repair itself, I caught the queen's wrist in my hand. She pushed with all her strength, inching closer to my exposed chest. The queen was strong where I was weak. My other hand grasped around her arm and slowly I began to twist and twist until her shoulder popped out of its socket. A loud screech echoed throughout the night as it roared from the queen's mouth. Leaping away from me and into the air, I breathed a heavy sigh of relief. My life could have ended right then. But I could not relish in relief for long, the battle was still waging.

    This battle I could not win alone. Glancing over, my eyes met with Desdemona's. She wanted to fight but she knew to stay away until I could no longer do this alone. If two of us went up against the queen, then we had a higher chance of winning. Desdemona would be the perfect choice, her training as a hunter would prove useful now. A nod of my head told her she may join the fight. Pointing my finger toward the sword that lay upon the ground, she knew what to do. As she rushed toward it, I leapt into the sky to confront the queen.

    Her shoulder had repaired itself, but I knew it still pained her. Lashing out, my nails scraped across her cheek. Four long gashes tore open her skin. Crimson dripped from the wounds and fell to the ground like a bloody rain. A mad chuckle escaped her as her hands attacked. Raising my arms, I blocked her hits. Still she continued her assault. Bruises whelped on my arms. Black and purple discolored my skin. But as soon as they appeared, they disappeared. My healing was like no other's. Much like the queen's. When she gifted me this life, she also gifted me half her strength and healing. Many of her abilities, I inherited from her bite and blood. Thus, making me her strongest child. Making me the only one to stand against her.

    My leg swooped out and smashed against her side, a bone in my foot broke but I cared not. The breath had been knocked from the queen's lungs, her eyes almost bulged from their sockets. Reaching out, my hand grasped around her throat, her nails scratched at my hand, and I hurtled her body through the sky. She too, slammed into the side of the castle, where I had been thrown. Her skull cracked against the stone and she slumped. Then, she fell. Down, down, down until she made contact with the ground. The earth caved in, the stone cracking around her. Vampires bodies were like rock, hard and heavy. A moan escaped the queen as she stood. Her body swayed. Scrapes danced across her pale skin. Crimson discolored it. But her wounds healed quickly.

    Still hovering within the sky, I glanced down to meet with Desdemona's waiting eyes. She was ready to make her attack. Tightly she gripped the hilt of the sword within her hands. As of now, her attack would fail. I needed to distract the queen, gain her attention, before Desdemona could deliver her fatal blow. Plummeting down from the sky, I aimed myself at the queen. She turned around to face me with a smile upon her lips. Stretching her arms out wide, she welcomed my attack. Our bodies collided but I was not the one to come out on top. Though I dealt out the attack, she had maneuvered herself in such a way that she had slipped from my grasp. And that was exactly what I wanted.

    A deranged laugh escaped her. Her eyes seemed crazed. "I told you, you could not defeat me! Now, I shall end your life! Never again shall you go against your queen!"

    Raising her hand into the air, I watched as if everything had slowed down around me. Slowly her sharpened nails inched toward my exposed chest. Part of me believed that I was to die here and now. Though I feared death, I welcomed it in this moment. Why? Because my soul would be freed. And perhaps all vampires weren't damned to the underworld. Maybe, just maybe there was a place for our souls to rest peacefully for all eternity. But would I choose that? Or would I choose to roam the lands and drift along the winds? Both seemed pleasing. Both seemed serene. No longer would I have to fight. No longer would I have to feel pain. I would be in a state of complete and utter bliss. And perhaps my lover would join me in the other world or join me along the wind. But today, was not my time. Today, I would live to see many more years.

"Desdemona, now!" My voice cried out my daughter's name.

A second later my eyes watched as the tip of the sword pierced through the queen's chest. Blood sprayed from the wound and splattered across my face. The queen's eyes grew wide. Crimson leaked from her perfect lips. A coughing fit seized her as she toppled over onto the stone ground. There she lay on her side, the sword piercing through her heart. Crimson pooling all around her. Soon her long, long life would come to an end. Her reign of cruelty would end as well. No longer would she be feared by her children. No longer would she deal out cruel and unnecessary punishments.

Desdemona approached the queen and slowly removed the sword that punctured her chest. Standing over the dying woman, she held the sword above her head. Today, the queen's execution would be dealt out. A painful, labored laugh sounded from the queen as she rolled over on her back to gaze upon Desdemona and I. Her heart was slowly healing, we needed to be quick with the execution.

"It seems as though I have been defeated by one of my own." She coughed up blood as she laughed once more. "Maybe you aren't as weak as I thought, my daughter."

"Goodbye, Persephone." Glancing over at Desdemona, I nodded my head to her.

The queen closed her eyes as the sword came down toward her neck. A smile plastered itself upon her lips and the sword sliced through her skin, splitting her bone, and off her head came. Blood spurted into the air and drizzled to the ground. The queen's life was over. As we stood over her dead body, it began to snow. Flurries fluttered down from the dark evening sky. They swirled around our beings and slowly began to pile atop the queen's corpse. Soon, she would be buried beneath the snow. Warmer weather never dared venture into these parts. The snow shall never melt away. Here her body would remain, imprisoned in snow from now till the end of time itself.

A New Queen Shall Reign

Chapter Fourteen

Vampires filtered into the courtyard. Their eyes beheld their fallen queen. Hushed whispers and gasps of shock trailed across the wind. It sounded within my ears. Many were enraged that their queen had been murdered. Many felt relief. I could feel their emotions mixing around within the air surrounding us. The anger swarmed like angry wasps. The relief washed over me like a cool ocean wave. My attunement to emotions was rather odd but I never questioned it.

Retracting my fangs, I stepped forth toward the confused crowd of vampires. They could not believe or understand why the queen's most adored child played a hand in her murder. Brows were raised in my direction. Though the vampires were angered, they would never dare attack me. For I was their new queen. None were brave enough to go against the former queen and none will be brave enough to go against I. A new queen shall reign. I would not rule with cruelness or fear. This queen shall rule in the areas the former queen had failed in.

    I raised my voice so that it may be heard across the land, "Tonight one queen's reign has ended and a new one has begun. I give each of you a choice, something the former queen has never given you before. Freedom to choose what you wish to do with your lives. Those who wish to remain here, may stay and know me to be their new queen. Those who wish to leave and travel the world, may do as they wish. If you ever decide to return, then the castle doors will be open and ready to welcome you back." Holding my chin up high I continued, "Your life is your own. Remember that."

    A hushed silence draped around the crowd of vampires. Their eyes stared upon me in wonder. Never have they been given freedom to do as they wish. All they have known was the queen's law. She controlled them and now they had a taste of freedom. A taste they did not know how to handle. Many would choose to stay, that much I knew. Some have never experienced freedom, they had grown too used to someone giving them orders.

    Finally, a few approached me. Though hesitation radiated from their aura, they knelt down to the ground before me. "Queen Nehemiah, we wish to remain here and know you as our new ruler." Soon, many more gathered before me. A few remained where they stood.

    Those few would choose freedom. They would roam faraway lands. Travel across distant seas. Fly through foreign skies. The world was there's. It rested within the palm of their hands. One of the few, was a servant girl. The same one that had to drag her friend's heartless body from the queen's chamber and dispose of her. I did not blame her for wishing to leave. The young vampire approached me, nervously.

    "Princess… I mean Queen Nehemiah. I wish to see my family. It's been years since I've talked to them."

    She flinched when I reached my arm toward her and placed my hand upon her shoulder. "Go. You are free to leave."

Tears swelled within her round blue eyes. "Thank you, my queen." She bowed her head to me and left the courtyard. Now, she would find her family. Now, she was free. The other few vampires followed in her footsteps and left this place.

Once the other vampires returned to the castle, it was only Selene, Desdemona, Nathaniel and I left alone in the courtyard. Still it snowed down upon us. Not like a blizzard but a gentle flurry. The snowflakes whisked along the wind and swirled around my being. The breeze rustled my long, dark locks. For once, it truly felt peaceful here. No longer would there be fear.

Turning my head, I glanced over at Desdemona. "My daughter, I ask you the same as I asked the others. Do you wish to remain here or travel the world?"

Her answer was instant. "Here I shall remain."

Nodding my head to her, I then turned my attention to Selene. "Now, I ask the same to you. Which do you choose?"

"I wish to remain here as well, and serve faithfully to you." She bowed.

Then, Nathaniel approached me. His clear blue eyes gazed upon me. A hint of pride radiated from his being. His hands found themselves around my waist. "Queen Nehemiah, my love, I choose to remain by your side. From now till the end of time." He smiled, creases formed around his ever clear eyes as the smile widened. The sweet smell of roses with a hint of honey perspired from his aura.

My hand cupped around my lover's cheek. Standing on my tip toes, I placed a tender kiss upon his sweet lips. "There is one thing I wish to do before I reign as queen."

He raised a brow to me. "And what would that be?"

Wrapping my arms around him, I stepped into his embrace. "I wish to travel the world with you. Like we had planned to so many years ago."

Gently grasping ahold on either side of my face, he peered down upon me. "I'll follow you wherever you go. I had promised you I would take you to see the world. And I will fulfill that promise."

"I love you, Nathaniel. More than I've ever loved anyone." My hand rested upon his and I pressed my cheek into his palm. The feel of his skin against mine felt so right.

"And I love you." Our lips met in a kiss of passion.

This is not Goodbye
Chapter Fifteen

Here we stood before the castle doors. Today, Nathaniel and I would depart. Together we would travel the world. Adventure across foreign lands. Soar through distant skies. We needn't take luggage with us on our journey. Vampires could easily get the things they wanted by using the sounds of our voices. We didn't know how long we would be gone or when we would return. All I know is that, this isn't goodbye. Someday we would return here. Then, I'll truly take my place as queen.

Desdemona approached us. A saddened look crossing her pretty face. My hand reached out and brushed a strand of curly, fiery hair behind her ear. "What troubles you?"

"When will you come back?"

"Perhaps years from now."

Her eyes were etched in despair. "So, this is goodbye?"

A smile crossed my lips as I embraced my daughter. "No. This is not goodbye. I promise to you that we shall return."

"I'll hunt you down if you don't." We both chuckled at her joke.

I grew serious for a moment. "Desdemona, while I am gone. I am leaving you in charge. I trust that you will take care of everyone for me. Selene shall help you, if you need her."

"I'll do my best."

"I trust that you will. After all, you are now the princess. This will you do some good to learn how to reign so that someday you might take my place as queen."

"And I hope it won't come down to a fight, like with the former queen."

"It won't."

My eyes caught sight of Selene as she rushed down the staircase. Her golden curls bounced through air. She bounded across the marble floor and launched herself at me. Her tiny arms wrapped around my body. "Don't think that I was going to let you leave without a hug." She winked a blue eye at me.

A laugh escaped my lips as I returned the embrace. "Do not miss me too much while I am gone."

"You're my favorite vampire here so of course I'll miss you!" She said in a whiny, choked voice.

My hand ruffled her golden curls. "Do good and help Desdemona if she needs it."

"I will, my queen." She bowed. It still was an odd feeling to hear someone call me queen.

Desdemona stepped forward, "Alright, we won't hold you two up any longer. Have safe travels."

"Take care, my daughter." With a smile I turned to face the door. Two vampire men approached them and pulled them open. Before our eyes lay a cold winter's night. Snow had blanketed the ground in its beauty. Nathaniel stood beside me. His hand rested on the lower of my back. We gazed into each other's eyes and stepped forward into the world. Once my foot crossed the threshold, I finally felt free. My life was mine once more.

As we traveled throughout the forest, my nostrils caught the scent of the wolf pack. It had seemed like forever since last I had saw them. There was one more thing I must do before I depart. Veering off deeper into the forest, Nathaniel followed close behind me. He did not question my sudden change of direction, he only followed quietly. Traveling the trail of the wolves' scent, I had finally found them. Carefully leaping into the top branch of a nearby tree, my eyes gazed down upon the wolves. I searched the clearing for the mother and her pups. Soon, I found them. And there playing amongst the others, was the pup I had given the mother. The pup I wished for her to care for, and she has. It dashed across the snowy ground chasing after three of the other young pups. It yipped and growled playfully. A chuckle escaped me as I watched it pounce through the air and tackle one of the pups. My heart was filled with happiness. Wolves were indeed my favorite animal. Strong, beautiful, and intelligent creatures they were. But my heart also swelled. So badly I had wanted to take the young pup under my care. But I could not tear it away from its family. Here it shall remain with the pack, where it belongs.

Nathaniel was seated beside me, his finger delicately wiped away the one tear from my cheek. "Go to it, Nehemiah. You'll regret it, if you don't."

I broke away from my lover's gaze and glanced down upon the pup. I wanted to hold it within my arms one last time before I left. Leaping down from the branch, my feet landed in the deep, frozen snow. The wolves were not startled by my sudden appearance. They knew me well. Just a few feet before me, was the pup. Its auburn eyes gazed upon me with curiosity. Adorably, it cocked its small head to the side. Kneeling down to the ground, I held my hand out toward it. A curious thing this pup was. It was not hesitant to approach me. It sniffed my fingers and rubbed its head against them. The pup's fur was so soft. My hand gently stroked the pup's back. Its tail waged happily. The wolf leapt into my lap and attacked my face with slobbery kisses. Laughter escaped from me. Oh, how I would dearly miss this young one. Though I wished to play with the pup longer, the mother approached me. It was time for the pack to leave. The pup gave me one last slobbery kiss before returning to its mother. It stood beneath her belly and waited for her to leave. The mother's eyes stared into mine.

"Thank you again, young mother."

The wolf nodded its head to me and turned around to leave. The rest of her pups followed close behind her as the pack left the clearing. Together they disappeared into the darkness of the forest. My heart began to ache. Nathaniel approached me, offering his hand to me I placed my hand into his palm. He lifted me from the snowy ground. Still holding my hand in his, he led me away from the clearing. He led me into a life of adventure.

As we left this place behind us, I held no regrets. It felt as though a weight had been lifted from my being. I felt light, free. Free to explore the world by my lover's side. My soul was enlightened. Eternal happiness filtered through my being. A smile spread across my lips as happy laughter escaped me. Nathaniel's emotions were the same as mine in this very moment. Together we would see the beauty this world has to offer. Long, long ago we had promised each other many things. One of them being; forever. And that very promise we would keep until the end of time itself.

Forever.

What is the meaning of eternal life without love?

To: Jeff and Iris

Brianna Paige
McClendon ♡

Made in the USA
Lexington, KY
16 June 2016